CHEERLEADERS®
#15

WAITING

JODY SORENSON

SCHOLASTIC INC.
New York Toronto London Auckland Sydney

To Mike

ISBN 0-590-40047-9

Copyright © 1986 by Jody Sorenson. All rights reserved. Published by Scholastic Inc.

12 11 10 9 8 7 6 5 4 3 2 1   3   6 7 8 9/8 0 1/9

Printed in the U.S.A.   01

CHEERLEADERS

WAITING

CHEERLEADERS

Trying Out

Getting Even

Rumors

Feuding

All the Way

Splitting

Flirting

Forgetting

Playing Games

Betrayed

Cheating

Staying Together

Hurting

Living It Up

Waiting

In Love

CHAPTER

Olivia Evans flipped from her stomach over onto her back, and onto her stomach again. Her mother was right about one thing. She *was* restless. And it wasn't just a matter of it being a warmer than usual day. Maybe that was part of it, but mostly she was bored. Plainly and simply bored.

"Olivia, shut that window! I can feel a draft all the way down to the end of the hall." A moment later her mother barged into her room. "B-r-r-r. You're far too thin to have your room this cold."

Olivia was tired of all the comments she got about her size. It was true she was tiny, but she had the perfect build for gymnastics, at which she excelled. "It's beautiful outside. Sunny and warmer than usual."

Her mother firmly shut the casement window. "It isn't spring yet. It's chilly. You'll catch your death of cold. I don't know what would happen

1

to you and your father if I wasn't around to protect you from your own foolishness."

"Yes, Mother." Olivia simply wanted her to leave and she'd agree to anything to have that happen.

"I fixed your favorite dinner. Ribs, real nice and spicy. When you see Walt at practice, invite him if you like. And put on your sweater when you go out."

"I know," Olivia muttered. "I don't want to catch my death of cold." As soon as her mother was down the hall, she leaped from her bed, opened the window, and breathed deeply, daring the pneumonia germs.

I'm bored, she thought. If I don't watch out, I'll catch my death of boredom. I need some kind of excitement. Something different.

"No," Walt Manners told Olivia when she tried to explain to him how she felt. "I haven't the faintest idea what you're talking about. I don't think your life is boring. And would you please close your window a little? This Jeep is breezy enough as it is."

"Spring is in the air, Walt. Can't you feel it?"

"You're too eager."

"Maybe. But it's seemed like such a long winter and I'm really ready for a change. Aren't you?"

"I like things the way they are. I've never minded winter. It's a cozy time."

"If you like being indoors."

Walt shrugged his broad shoulders. He lived in

a lovely home in the woods. It was special, original, with the atmosphere of a cozy cabin, yet modern, with glass and chrome. His parents lived a life of up-to-date action, always exploring new ideas for their early morning TV show. "What's wrong with being indoors?" he asked.

"My mother." They both laughed. "Well, at least you understand *something*," she said.

"What's that supposed to mean?"

"Your parents like you, really like you. They trust your judgment. Everybody does. People who don't know me look at how small I am and think I'm about twelve. Maybe ten," she said, exasperated. "And that's how they treat me. But I'm almost an adult, you know. And once people hear about my heart surgery when I was a kid, they treat me like I might expire any minute if I exert myself too much. Like I've still got some big physical defect. And don't you say a word about that being true, even to joke."

Walt raised his hand in protest. He'd never joke about someone's sore points, especially with Olivia, who was always proving just how physically fit she was, scaring even him — who was not only her boyfriend but also her cheerleading partner — with just how daring she could be in a routine. "You're being too sensitive. Everyone on the squad thinks you're great. There's no one more physically fit than you. Everybody who sees you perform agrees with that."

"I've got to do something exciting, Walt. Something with more of a challenge."

"You're plenty of excitement for me." He

3

turned toward her with a big smile and then looked back at the road ahead, as they made their last turn toward Angie Poletti's, where the squad was having a special Sunday afternoon practice. "Just don't do anything foolish, okay? People do foolish things for a thrill. I don't want you ending up dead."

"You're just like my mother." She hopped out of the Jeep and headed up the sidewalk.

"I am not!" he shouted, slamming shut the Jeep door. "You worry me, Olivia Evans," he muttered.

"Hey!" Pres Tilford shouted each time a member of the squad came through Angie's front door. "Claudia's coming home Wednesday. Isn't that great?" Claudia Randall was Pres's latest girl friend. Technically, Tarenton wasn't her home. She was from Virginia and had come to the area seeking medical attention for her spine, damaged in a fall from a horse. She finally decided to go to California for necessary, but life-threatening, surgery. Now she was coming back to Tarenton.

Pres had been the first to arrive at Angie's, Olivia and Walt, next. So by the time everyone had gathered, Olivia felt she had heard enough of Claudia's imminent arrival. "We know already, Pres. You've told us about a million times. She's all recovered. That's great. Now can't we get to work?"

"What's got into you?" Pres asked, looking over Olivia's head to Walt for an explanation.

4

"All I said — Hey, aren't you excited about Claudia coming home? I'd think after all the hospitalizations you've been through — "

"Olivia's excited about the weather," Walt interrupted.

"You and Ben," said Nancy Goldstein, pulling her long dark hair away from her face, making her exotic features even more eye-catching. "Now he can't wait for baseball. One sport after the other. He's a real jock," she described her boyfriend, Ben Adamson, a star basketball player at Tarenton.

"I am not like Ben," said Olivia, her large eyes widening and looking straight at Nancy.

"Did I say you were?" Nancy asked.

"That's exactly what you said," Olivia answered, tossing off her sweater. She was looking for excitement and here she was with the same old group of friends. She was beginning to feel bored with everything, including them. Claudia Randall's coming home didn't help at all. Everything Claudia had been through — going to a special hospital in California, being away from home, seeing specialist after specialist, finally having surgery that defied great odds — she had endured as a child. She hated thinking about it and Claudia only reminded her of that time. People expected her to relate to that kind of thing. Well, she wasn't in the mood to relate to Claudia.

Nancy looked at Walt. He merely shrugged. "Sorry," Nancy said. "You're awfully touchy, Olivia."

"Nancy is right," Pres said. "I get the best news I've had in ages and all you can do is muck it up. You're a real thorn in my side, Olivia." Pres, the only son of the town's wealthiest family, poked at his ribs beneath his pale yellow cashmere sweater to imitate a thorn and then laughed at his own joke. When no one laughed, he half rolled his deep blue eyes and ran his fingers through his dark blond hair. It was easy to tell that he found Olivia very exasperating that afternoon.

"You know, Pres," Olivia responded, "I don't care about your problems. As far as I can tell you have a life that gleams with as much success as the hottest commercial on TV."

"What'd you do?" Pres whispered in Walt's direction. "Feed her some tiger juice on your way over here?"

Walt shrugged. He knew when to stay quiet.

Just then Mary Ellen Kirkwood, their captain, breezed through the door. "Hey, Walt. This routine you wrote out for me is great." She quickly looped her long blonde hair through a rubber band and pulled it into a ponytail. Ponytail or not, Mary Ellen looked as if she had just stepped from the cover of a fashion magazine. "Wait till you guys try it out."

"Claudia's coming home Wednesday," Pres said so quickly that Mary Ellen didn't understand what he was saying. Besides, he had made everyone — everyone, that is, except Olivia — laugh.

"That's great, Pres," she said when she finally understood.

6

"Yeah, and I'm having a big party for her. To celebrate her recovery. It's an absolute miracle, as far as I'm concerned."

Everyone spent time then asking Pres questions about Claudia: what her recovery would be like, whether the problem with her spinal column was cured or if she'd require constant medical attention. Angie wanted to know if Claudia would ever get on a horse again. One question Pres couldn't answer definitely, though it was easy to tell how he wanted it answered, was whether she'd be staying in Tarenton. The Randalls were a wealthy family from Virginia and Claudia's stay in Tarenton had supposedly been only temporary.

Well, Olivia thought as she tried not to listen, there had better be something exciting to do soon or I'm going to go crazy with all these boring medical bulletins about the state of Claudia Randall's health.

CHAPTER

"Claudia arrived this afternoon and look where I have to be!" Pres scanned the high gym walls and then stared at Angie as if he couldn't quite believe the energy with which she was practicing cartwheels, her long blonde hair dusting the floor and then falling down around her shoulders as she stood. A moment later he flopped down on the floor next to Nancy and began to do push-ups. Walt and Olivia — always the earlybirds — were just finishing limbering up with the end segment from Walt's routine that was an imitation of a favorite rock video.

"Do you think any of us wants to be here?" Nancy asked, lying down on her back as if completely overcome with lethargy and then breaking into a quick series of sit-ups. "I'd like to be out bike riding with Ben."

"Hey, that sounds like fun," Pres said. "I bet Claudia would love something like that." He thought for a second. Biking was not high on his list of fun activities, but he did know that Tarenton had great bike paths. "If I can find enough to keep her entertained," he said, thinking aloud, "she'll *have* to stay in Tarenton."

"Claudia isn't exactly going to be in shape for anything too exciting," Olivia said.

"Maybe you should go easy," Nancy suggested. "For a while, anyway."

"No," Pres said. "I haven't gotten the impression Claudia wants to take it easy. She says she's determined to get back to being her old self. Right away. I've gotten several letters from her and — "

"Ooooh, love letters," squealed Angie, just to tease Pres. She threw her arms around him.

Pres smiled. "Well, maybe we'll have to take it easier than I think. But nothing can beat a spin around the lake in the Porsche." The red Porsche that had been a birthday gift from his folks was Pres's most prized possession.

"That would get her blood moving, all right," Nancy said with that tone of hers that always got a laugh.

"And make her hair stand on end," Angie joked.

"Give her a kiss from me," Walt said. "That'll get her blood moving."

"I've already started planning the party," Pres said. "The biggest bash you guys have ever seen."

Olivia avoided Walt's gaze. A party, even at the Tilfords', was definitely not the exciting thing she hoped to find right around the corner.

*　*　*

In the locker room after practice Pres wiped his face with a towel, the oversized cherry and white striped towel that was his father's favorite. His dad had been looking for it for over a month now, sure one of the help had misplaced it just to annoy him. Annoying his dad was something Pres was good at, whether or not that was what he was trying to accomplish. By becoming a cheerleader Pres had caused his father no end of frustration and irritation.

Pres was so anxious to see Claudia that any delay seemed intolerable. He got into the shower and lathered up in ten seconds, rinsed in ten more, thinking about Claudia every second.

She hadn't wanted Pres to meet her at the airport and disrupt his schedule. "Come see me as soon as you're free," she'd said during their last phone call. "I can take care of myself. You just save your strength for me. And we'll get right back to where we left off."

It was clear to Pres, even if it wasn't to anyone else, that Claudia was making every effort to be her bold, carefree self, exactly what had attracted him to her in the first place. Her energetic, fiery spirit and her big violet eyes fascinated him. He'd have a homecoming party perfectly suited to her, a party the likes of which his parents' estate had never, in its decades of affluence, witnessed. It would be the biggest bash any of his friends had ever seen. And he hoped it would even be enough to cement Claudia's interest in making Tarenton her home.

10

Pres raced up the porch steps to the front door of Dr. Harroldson's residence, where Claudia was staying, a bunch of bright yellow daisies in his fist. He just about broke the door down in his excitement to get to her.

"Pres," she said, her slight southern drawl making his name sound at once sweet and sexy.

She looks fine, Pres decided immediately. Claudia's presence affected him the way it always had, as if his breath was being stopped at the top of his chest.

She made his pulse quicken and warmed every nerve. Her surgery hadn't changed anything. Quickly he took her in his arms, roughly shoving away the part of his brain that was calculating the nature of Claudia's condition. He didn't want her to be any different from before. But his concern kept coming back. "Am I holding you too tight?" he asked.

Maybe he shouldn't hold her so he'd put any pressure on her spine, he thought. Her fingertips' touch against his cheek seemed a little cooler than before. He certainly didn't want her to catch a cold. Pneumonia — that got a lot of people after they'd almost completely recovered from serious surgery.

He scooped her up and carried her to the sofa, setting her down gently, carefully smoothing the mammoth rose afghan that lay in a heap in the middle of the sofa over her legs. "How are you feeling?"

"Oh, Pres, it is *so* good to see you. It's been like a drought to be without you. I'm fine. Don't worry about me, at least not that way. If you want to play doctor, prescribe kisses, please."

"Please" came out in two syllables and Pres laughed.

She murmured, "You have no idea how good it feels to hear a laugh. No one around me laughs. Or makes me laugh. I guess they're afraid that on top of everything else I'll burst my appendix or something."

"You won't, will you?"

"Of course not."

Pres sat back, relaxing against the sofa's gold brocade, Claudia's legs in his lap. "Did you meet any cute doctors?"

"Tons."

"I was afraid of that."

"California's full of cute people. You get used to it."

"Speak for yourself."

She laughed. "I know. You'd relish an opportunity like that. I thought about how you'd act out there and it pulled me through many a dull moment. I was glad you were waiting for me here in safe little Tarenton, though your trip to New York made me a little nervous. Not that the folks in Tarenton are ugly, mind you."

"No, definitely not ugly," he said to tease her.

"It was more the atmosphere. You have no idea how many times I planned a car trip for us, down the Coast Highway, taking the curves in your Porsche, the ocean like diamonds." Her violet eyes sparkled.

There *is* something different about her, Pres

thought. She seems gentler, softer. "You're different," he said.

"Oh, don't you tell me that, too. I'm the same. I just have to watch a few things."

"Like what? I don't want you keeping any secrets about your physical condition. I want to take good care of you — better than you'd get anywhere else."

"Oh, all I really need is to be with you. I could be with you till I die."

He could see her eyes fill with tears as she mentioned the idea of dying. He squeezed her hands. "But you didn't die."

"I'm so very thankful," she murmured, trying to force her quivering lips into a smile. "I came so close. I even think I was ready to die. It was hard not knowing, not having any certainty about the outcome of the operation."

"I always knew." Really, though, Pres hadn't. He didn't like not knowing outcome any more than Claudia, especially when it had to do with death, and he didn't want to upset her more than she already was. And he didn't want to cry himself, even tears of gratitude.

"You gave me the strength I needed, Pres, lots of times. I'd think about what you were up to, what you were thinking." Suddenly, she gasped, startling him.

"What's the matter?" he asked quickly.

"My mom! She's in the den. I made her promise to stay in there till we'd had a chance to talk. And she was not to eavesdrop."

"Your mom would hold to a promise like that?"

"I glued my Walkman to her eardrums."

When Claudia's mother came into the room Pres said, "Well, I can tell who Claudia takes after. I mean the beauty part and all."

"Nicely put, young man. You have a delightful way with words. Claudia told me you were poetic."

Mrs. Randall reached out her hand and Pres took it, aware then of the gold bracelets that jangled at her wrist and diamonds dazzling her fingers. "Poetic?" he asked.

Claudia laughed. "That's how I explained the cheerleading to her. In the south, men don't do that sort of thing too much, but it's all right to be poetic."

"You don't look poetic at all," said Mrs. Randall, openly admiring Pres's build.

Pres thought he might blush for the first time in his life. Poetic he certainly wasn't. At the moment he could hardly get his tongue in gear. "I hope you're enjoying your time here in Tarenton." He certainly didn't want Mrs. Randall persuading her daughter to return to Virginia.

Mrs. Randall arched her brows and laughed. "I try not to intrude in Claudia's affairs. I let her use her good sense and this is where she wanted to come to recuperate. In return she doesn't intrude on me. I only came to get her settled and to visit with the Harroldsons for a while. I head off for a little sun in Jamaica Saturday morning. Isn't this weather ghastly?"

14

Pres wanted to protest that Claudia needed her mother, but then he really didn't know her situation fully. He wanted her to be well, and if she was well enough for her mother to jet off to some vacation island, then fine. He looked at Claudia, but found no clue as to whether her mother's departure was good or disappointing. Well, he'd take good care of her. "Actually, the weather's getting better. But the weather doesn't really matter to me."

"You're lucky," Mrs. Randall said.

"Yeah. I'm going to be spending time with Claudia. It could blizzard for a solid week, and I wouldn't care." He smiled at Claudia and reached for her hand.

Finally, he'd found someone. Well, not just *someone*. He'd found the girl of his dreams, she was alive, and the whole world was going to celebrate.

The cheerleaders were in high spirits for the game two nights later with Kensington. The Kensington Kings weren't a piece of cake, but they usually made Tarenton look like a professional team by comparison. And the cheerleaders always ended up giving a stunning performance, too.

"Ben's terrific tonight," Nancy said as he stole the ball from Sam Bell, captain of the Kings, and a split second later did a slam dunk that left everyone screaming for more.

"I'd say you're prejudiced," Angie said.

"Just a little," Nancy admitted with a big

smile. She had never felt so happy. It was the kind of happiness that didn't really seem to have a source, a reason.

Of course, she thought, if I really want to figure out *why* I should feel so happy, I could. I have plenty of reasons. Ben Adamson, Tarenton's newest basketball player and already the team's star, was at the top of her list. They'd dated for a while — she felt warmth inch across her face, reminding her just how strongly they'd been attracted to each other from the very beginning — when he was captain of the Garrison team. When he transferred to Tarenton all her daydreams came to life. She'd never find anyone as able to hold all her attention as Ben. He was never dull, and always made her smile and laugh. When he held her, she felt the world could never be better or more fun. He just had everything. "Legs," she shouted.

"What?" Angie asked.

"Nothing," said Nancy as she bent forward, elbows on knees, to watch the game and to hide her embarrassment at blurting out one of her nicknames for Ben.

"I heard," Angie said. "I heard something about legs." She gave Nancy's elbow a playful shove that knocked Nancy off balance and about landed her head-first inbounds.

The two girls giggled, and then grew serious as Sam Bell was fouled and earned two free throws. Tarenton was so far ahead then, near the end of the second half, that the Tarenton home crowd even gave Sam near-quiet for his free throws. He made one, narrowing the Tarenton lead to fifteen points.

The six cheerleaders flew out onto the court, Pres swinging Nancy up to his broad, white-sweatered shoulders; Walt yelling into the shiny red megaphone with TARENTON WOLVES lettered in white; while Olivia cartwheeled through the air, a blaze of red and white as she flipped from end to end. Mary Ellen used her pompons to get the Tarenton fans to their feet; Angie doing leaps and arches that set her long blonde hair flying and her red wool skirt with its white pleats swinging.

"More! More! More!
Take the floor! More! More! More!
Take the floor and raise that score!"

Tarenton won by twelve points, even with the second string in for the last few minutes.

I have everything, Nancy thought as she hugged Angie, and then Mary Ellen, and searched the floor for Ben. He almost always raced up with a sweaty kiss, win or lose.

"Gotcha," Ben said.

Nancy looked up at him. No one, no one ever, would make her happier than Ben.

"You two," Angie said, "look lost on Mars."

Ben gave Nancy a kiss. "We're right here, Ange. And I'm scanning the crowd for the perfect guy for you." He put his hand to his brow, searching the crowd, his mouth a serious frown, his eyes squinting.

17

"Don't bother," Angie said. It had been a while since she and Arne Peterson had decided to be "just friends," but she still wasn't used to being without a boyfriend. "I want what the two of you have, nothing less. And it's not here. I've taken a good look."

"There won't be anyone but the squad at my party tonight," said Nancy. "I didn't invite anyone else."

"Good," Angie said. "I've been looking forward to it all week. Just to end this pointless searching for the perfect man. So I'll be the only one there without a date. So what?"

Nancy and Ben looked at her without saying a word.

"So I'll eat you out of house and home, that's so what." When Nancy and Ben laughed, Angie went on. "I am really glad the party's just for us cheerleaders. You know, everything's finally going so well for all of us that it will really feel good to be together. You know, comfortable and fun."

CHAPTER

"I think I need to sit down," Claudia said soon after she and Pres arrived at Nancy's party.

Pres reached for her. She seemed to slip right into his arms, light as a bird. He didn't hesitate a second before leaving the conversation about the professional basketball season that he was having with Patrick Henley, Mary Ellen's on-again, off-again boyfriend. As far as Pres could tell, the nature of the Kirkwood-Henley romance depended solely on how Patrick's garbage collecting business was affecting Mary Ellen's image of herself. Pres was glad Claudia never played that game with him.

"Are you all right?" he asked her. She looked all right, now that he had her tucked into a corner of the Goldsteins' nubby beige sofa, but he wanted to make sure.

"Tired, I guess. A party and a game — it's all

19

too much." She smiled up at him. "I guess right now it's hard to know how much I can do."

Once she smiled that smile of hers Pres knew she was okay. "It must be. Don't strain yourself. I want you healthy for *my* party."

"Another party? I'll never make it, Pres, honey."

"Not tonight." He thought of calling her "honey," too. Claudia and her mom used the term all the time, rich with a southern accent. "Honey" fit in some circles, not in others. Pres wasn't quite comfortable with the word.

"I've got one planned for after next week's game with Garrison. A real 'Welcome home, Claudia' party."

Just then Vanessa Barlow, the school superintendent's dark-haired daughter, came through the front door. She had in tow Nat Harris, one of the best defensive basketball players on the team and Ben Adamson's best friend. Everyone noticed, because Vanessa, who had tried out for cheerleading and failed, and who had made revenge her purpose in life ever since, was definitely *not* invited to Nancy's party. It was strictly a party for the cheerleaders and their dates, and the atmosphere in the living room reflected that: cozy, fun, and intimate.

Until Vanessa walked in. Immediately, conversations and laughter froze.

"Hey, Ben!" Nat Harris called out. "Thanks for mentioning the party to me. It got me a date with Vanessa here. Where's the food? That was some game, wasn't it?"

Everyone — everyone, that is, except Claudia — turned toward Nancy. She shrugged her shoulders. She wouldn't fight what had happened. Nancy hated a scene just about as much as she hated Vanessa Barlow. Vanessa was the last person she wanted at her party, which was exactly why Vanessa had come. Nat Harris was not Vanessa's type, but she would date any man if he got her what she wanted and where she wanted to go.

"Vanessa," Claudia said softly to Pres. "I remember her."

"And I remember *you*," Vanessa said, eagerly taking a seat on the sofa next to Claudia. "I'm here to welcome you home, like everyone else."

Pres clenched his fists. Vanessa really got under his skin when she put on her goody-goody tone of voice. But at least Vanessa, with her phony sort of graciousness, was making a fuss over Claudia. And more than anything, Pres wanted her to feel at home in Tarenton.

While Vanessa snuggled up to Claudia and began to talk, Pres headed toward Patrick who, along with Ben, was making himself a sandwich from the spread of cold cuts in the dining room.

"I don't think Winchester Peak would be that difficult," Ben was saying. "The route up the west side is rated a five-five. It's a one day climb, easily. And the bad weather is definitely over. There's old snow up there, but that's part of the challenge, isn't it?"

"Five-point-five or not, there's one good stretch of technical climbing along that route," Patrick said, stabbing at the stack of salami. "Have you ever made that climb?"

"No, but it can't be any more difficult than Mt. Heritage. And I did that by myself last spring."

"You shouldn't climb alone," Patrick said.

"I know. But I'm as nimble and steady as they come. Nothing bad happened." Ben spread out his arms to make the point that he was there, all in one piece. The thin-sliced turkey that was caught in the prongs of the fork he held in his right hand dropped to the floor.

"I hope you're a better mountain climber than a sandwich maker," Pres said as he bent down and tossed the meat onto Ben's plate.

"I climb only slightly less skillfully than I play basketball."

Pres and Patrick smiled broadly. "The guy's real modest," Pres said.

"How about it, Patrick?" Ben persisted. "We could make the climb next Saturday. With an early start we'd be back in plenty of time for the game."

"How could you do both?" Pres asked. "You've got to be in top shape for the game. Everyone counts on you now. I don't know what we did before you transferred to Tarenton."

"The game's with Garrison. I can play them with my eyes shut and my knee in a brace," Ben said, recalling his days with Garrison.

Patrick shrugged. "If you think so. The weather's a bit unpredictable right now, though."

"Are you chicken?" Ben asked. "On a mountain the weather's always unpredictable. Rain clouds come and go."

"What's there to be chicken about?" Olivia wanted to know, as she reached out for a nibble of the chocolate cheesecake that crowned the selection of desserts at one end of the table.

Pres wished Olivia hadn't joined them. "This is men's talk," he said instantly.

Patrick laughed. "I thought we were all through with distinctions between the sexes. After all, anybody can be chicken. Men and women."

"Not Olivia," said Pres. "She's never chicken."

Olivia seemed to perk up at Pres's description of her. "Depends," she said. "I don't like the dark."

"We're talking about climbing Winchester Peak," Ben explained. "In daylight. At least that's when I do my climbing. You don't have a night climb in mind, do you, Patrick?"

"Are you kidding?"

Olivia was intrigued. She'd taken a rock climbing class two summers ago, but hadn't had much of a chance to practice what she'd learned. She'd give just about anything to be climbing with Patrick and Ben. She'd hardly imagined anything that exciting happening. "Are you guys talking about a climb anytime soon?"

"We haven't made definite plans," Ben answered. Mayonnaise oozed from the edges of the large rye bread dagwood he'd concocted during the past ten minutes, as he gave it a good squeeze to fit it into his mouth. "I sure would like to climb Winchester Peak next Saturday, though. Maybe we could publicize it as a way of beginning a mountain climbing club at school. There are enough mountains around here to start something like that, you know. Are you interested?" Ben began to eat his sandwich with great relish.

"Sure," Olivia said. "I took a course two summers ago," she explained. "We did a lot of hiking and rock climbing. Mountain survival, too. I know I could climb Winchester Peak. Our instructor called me a lightweight mountain goat and said I was the best student he'd had in ages. And I'm strong," she quickly added. She looked from Ben to Patrick.

Climbing with Ben and Patrick seemed just the shot in the arm she needed to get some invigorating excitement into her life. "Come on, Patrick. Let's do it."

"Your mom will kill you," Pres said.

"My mom has nothing to do with this. It's between Patrick, Ben, and me. It's whether the guys trust me as a mountain climbing partner."

"You'd be great to have along," Patrick said right away. "And there's no reason a mountaineering club at school would be just for guys. Besides, a climbing party should have three members, minimum. That's one of the rules."

"Everybody takes courses. But what exactly do you know?" Ben asked Olivia. "I mean, we'd depend on you just like a guy. I know you're a cheerleader and all, but you don't look that strong. No offense."

Olivia was not hurt by the remark. Ben was

being honest and she respected that in him. Mountain climbing was serious business and it was wise to question your partners. Objective things went into climbing, like level of skill; and subjective things, like whether you could rely on another's judgment and maturity. Olivia went through what she'd done in the rock climbing and survival class she'd taken. "Rock climbing isn't easy, you know," she said.

"No," Ben said. "And you've done more than me." He went on to explain the peaks in the vicinity that he'd climbed. "I guess I can't complain about having you along, Olivia."

"Olivia's a skilled gymnast," Patrick said. "After what I've heard, I haven't a worry. And she's smart. That counts for a lot in the event something happens."

"Nothing's going to happen," Ben said. "With us three it'll go smooth as a summer's breeze. I guarantee it."

News of the climb traveled quickly through the small party, the climbers protesting that they'd be back in time for Ben to rest up for the game with Garrison and go on to win it. Everyone else was concerned about the wisdom of their plan.

"You'd be lucky if Pres were joining the climb," Vanessa told Claudia.

"Why's that?"

"It just might burn up some of his devilish energy and make him settle down. I'm sure you know all about Pres by now. There must be a million stories about how wild he is, disappearing for days, racing his car around the lake, sometimes even getting his friends into trouble. He means well. He can't help himself, I guess. His freedom and having fun come first."

"We both like freedom. It's part of the attraction, don't you think?"

"Maybe. If you like losing Pres to other women." Vanessa watched Claudia swallow hard. "I don't mean to scare you."

"There's very little that scares me anymore. And, really, Pres is different with me."

"That's what they all say."

"He's very caring. He's giving me a party next Saturday, after the game. Just a little welcome home party."

"Pres?" Vanessa shouted. "A *little* party? You should see the parties he gives. They last all night. It'll be a wild time, if I know Pres."

"Maybe you don't know him," Claudia said.

"Oh, I know Pres Tilford *very* well." Vanessa took this turn in their conversation as her cue to leave, swinging her head the way she used to. She always forgot her hair had been cut for the New York commercial at moments like this.

Pres, seeing that Claudia was being freed from the clutches of Vanessa, headed in her direction. But he simply could not avoid Vanessa.

"Pres, honey," Vanessa whispered into his ear in a southern accent that was full of mockery for Claudia. "Claudia is starting to fade and thinks she needs to go home. I think she looks ghostly, don't you? Or would ghastly be a better description?"

26

Pres clenched a fist. "That's better than *being* ghastly. Which is what you are."

Vanessa threw back her head and laughed. "Anything you say, Pres, honey." Then she headed toward the group that was still discussing next Saturday's climb of Winchester Peak.

"You and Olivia are good friends, aren't you?" Mary Ellen asked Patrick. Now that Nancy's party was over and she and Patrick were heading home, she could say what had been on her mind the past few hours. Nancy's party had been fun, somehow more fun than most. And everyone had gotten silly. She and Angie had done old dances, giggling as if they were at one of their junior high slumber parties.

But when Patrick had danced with Olivia, things hadn't felt like quite so much fun. After all the talk about mountain climbing, and knowing how Patrick had been friendly with Olivia in the past — well, Mary Ellen had gotten this uneasy feeling that if she didn't watch out she'd end up a third wheel. Though she knew she was the one, and not Patrick, who controlled their relationship.

Patrick glanced over at her with one of his I-know-what's-eating-you smiles, his eyes ready to laugh and tease. "You're jealous."

Mary Ellen felt herself stiffen in defense. Maybe she was jealous, but she really couldn't afford to have even that strong a feeling about Patrick. She enjoyed his company, but she didn't want to admit to more. She didn't want him to put a claim on her, or mess up the dream she had of becoming a model with a glorious life in New York. After all, who would want to trade that kind of life to stay in Tarenton and spend decades with Patrick and his garbage truck? Even if he had more sex appeal than anyone she'd ever met or seen? But lately, it seemed she couldn't do without him. And she wasn't about to share him, or lose him. "Jealous of you and Olivia? Not in the least."

"Then why are you interested in whether Olivia and I are pals?"

"Well, are you?"

"Sure. I like Olivia. But not the way I like you."

Mary Ellen was thinking maybe the way Patrick liked Olivia was better somehow than the way he liked her. "You like doing the same kinds of things. Athletic kinds of things. I don't have the faintest idea how to do that rappeling thing she was talking about. Would you enjoy mountain climbing with me as much as with her?"

"*We* enjoy doing a lot of other things that I'd never even dream of doing with Olivia. Why do we have to mountain climb, too?"

"One could lead to the other."

Patrick laughed. "You're not interested in sharing mountain climbing with me, are you? You're worried whether a mountain climb with Olivia might lead to a kiss. Tell the truth, Mary Ellen."

"Why not? Olivia's a girl. You're a boy."

"If you're so concerned, why don't you come along?"

"I don't know the first thing about all that technical stuff you were talking about. I'd just slow you down."

"Maybe that would be for the best. I'm not all that keen on wearing Ben out for the game. If that happens, my name will be mud. That game with Garrison is really important for our standing in the district. The three of us could teach you a lot about climbing in a day. Even in half a day."

"Then *I'd* be responsible for wearing Ben out. No thanks. To tell you the truth, I don't think I'm really interested in hard core mountain climbing. Besides, I have to work at Marnie's Saturday morning." Mary Ellen sighed. "I just don't know what's wrong with me. I guess I don't like the idea of the climb. It sounds too difficult, especially right before a game."

"I've got the cure for what ails you." He pulled his truck over to the curb. An instant later his lips were against hers. He kissed her lightly, gently. His fingers caressed her cheeks and neck. It seemed he always read her mood right. He soothed her, all her worry evaporating. Almost.

CHAPTER

"Thanks for staying to help clean up," Nancy said to Ben, as he slid the remains of the chips into a plastic bag. "You must be exhausted."

"Yeah. Sometimes it's hard to party after a game. But not tonight. You look special for some reason. I guess that's what's keeping me up."

"I do?"

"Yeah. There's extra color in your cheeks. And something about your eyes, too."

"Well, I like giving parties."

"You must." Just as she was about to put the thin-sliced ham back in its wrapping, he scooped her into his arms. "You're some kind of woman, Nancy."

She melted. Lately, she was feeling like a woman. Not so much a girl anymore. She wondered if Ben had noticed the difference or if calling her a "woman" was just an accident. The way he was holding her made her feel he had

30

noticed. Special? Maybe that's what was special about her. "I feel like a woman with you."

"Mmmm, I like the sound of that." He nuzzled her neck and tightened his hold around her slim waist.

Nancy closed her eyes. Now, if someone would just come and turn out the kitchen light. She figured she could live in Ben Adamson's arms for the rest of her life. Right then, he lifted her off her feet and carried her toward the living room. "I know where you're headed, Adamson. My parents have ears like elephants."

"Goldstein, don't I know it. And eyes like eagles. They were young once. They have to remember what it's like. Besides, after all your hard work putting together the party, you deserve a little relaxation."

Nancy almost giggled as he tossed her back onto the sofa. But a giggle didn't fit, really. She had always been thrown a little by the feeling between them. "There will never be anyone like you, Ben," she whispered against his lips as they kissed.

"There better not be." Their kiss transformed ... mile, back into a kiss. "I'll love you for-

into a s... ever,

t's good enough for me." Nancy knew
isn't joking about loving her forever. He
ense like that. She felt the warm palm of
d against the flesh of her waistline. She
ow he kissed and held her, though at first
constant affectionate nature had made her
uncomfortable. She had told him about it, about

31

wanting to talk sometimes, and so sometimes they did talk.

She kissed his neck, his cheek, his forehead. Her hand brushed back his hair that was always slightly uncombed. Ben was daring one minute, boyishly cute the next. They had a passionate connection and Nancy wouldn't change either part of him. And yet, sometimes he did worry her.

"I want to talk," she said.

"Not *now*!"

"Well, we don't have to sit up." It was already too late. Ben was sitting on the edge of the sofa.

"I can't talk and kiss at the same time," he said. "You should know that by now."

"Other people do."

"What other people do you have in mind?"

"On TV. In the movies."

"Kissing is like basketball for me. There's only one thing on my mind."

"I know exactly what's on your mind. That's why I want to talk."

"We've already talked about that. You're in charge."

"So that's why we're talking. I just do[n't like] the idea of you mountain climbing next Sat[urday]. You've got a real chance at a good baske[tball] scholarship. What if that's the game the recrui[ters] from the university come to watch and you're n[ot] playing as well as usual? What if you pull a muscle or something?"

"You heard Patrick. He's not about to get that adventurous."

32

"You attract adventure like flowers attract bees."

"Nancy, we're just going on a little climb. The first of the season. To get our legs in gear. I'm in great physical shape. Need I remind you of that?"

"No."

"I'll do fine. I'll do better than fine. That outdoor air will only invigorate me. And I need a change of pace. I love basketball, but there's more to life than shooting baskets. And if I don't get a scholarship, so what? I've got the money to go without a scholarship, and I'll play college basketball whether I'm on a scholarship or not. Don't worry. I'm in fine company with Patrick and Olivia. They're really knowledgeable. Did you hear Olivia talking about what she knows?"

"I heard. She's a good athlete for cheerleading. But mountain climbing? She's so tiny."

"Jealous?"

"No. Not really." Nancy paused. "But if she gets any ideas. . . ."

"Come here and I'll give you that very opportunity." He pulled her toward him and he started kissing her again as if it was a life or death proposition.

"Why do you want to go and do something as silly as climbing Winchester Peak?" Walt had never been so upset. Olivia was acting stranger than strange lately. And now mountain climbing. "And right before the game with Garrison. Are you nuts or something? What are you trying to prove? That you're an Amazon? I didn't know you knew the first thing about mountain climbing. You're driving me crazy, Olivia. Something about this is not right. You're a girl."

"Girls climb. A group of women climbed Annapurna."

"Yeah. I heard about that. And two of them didn't come back."

She was sorry she'd mentioned Annapurna, though it had been a glorious event for women climbers. "Winchester Peak isn't the least bit like the Himalayas."

"Anything can happen on a climb."

"If it was too dangerous, the guys wouldn't be doing it. It was their idea in the first place. Not mine."

"So that doesn't mean you have to go along with it. At least promise me one thing," he said, reaching over to take her hand. "If you have any doubts at all about the wisdom of this climb, you'll decide not to go. Even if it's at the last minute. I'd help you come up with something to save face."

She squeezed his hand. "Thanks, Walt. I'm not changing my mind. But it's nice to know you'd be on my side."

"I'm on your side, either way." He did love her.

Walt pressed on the accelerator and shifted into fourth gear, ready to drive to their favorite parking place by the lake.

"I've been thinking, Pres," Claudia said. "Of going home."

34

"Home?" He had been expecting something like this, worrying about it, but he was still stunned.

"Back to Virginia."

"What for?"

"Well, it *is* home. I might be safer there. You know, recuperate better."

"Is that why your mother came to visit? To get you to come home? I wish you'd told me."

"No," said Claudia slowly, turning away from him toward the big picture window in Dr. Harroldson's living room where they were saying a long good-night after Nancy's party. "Actually, it was my talk with Vanessa."

Pres was even more stunned. "Vanessa? What does she have to do with it? She doesn't know the first thing about people getting well. All she has to do is breathe on something and it shrivels."

"She seems very energetic to me."

"Yeah. About all the wrong things. Like convincing you to go back to Virginia. What about me? I'm the best medicine you could ever take."

Claudia didn't laugh. She smiled and brushed away a tear.

Pres reached out and took her in his arms. She didn't resist.

"This is why I think I should go home. So I'm ready for you and your wild ways."

"Wild ways? I'm me. Pres Tilford."

"Oh, don't try to hide it, Pres. It's why we connected in the first place. We both like action. But I'm having to face the fact that I need to slow down. The surgery's over, but I'm not like I was. For a while I have to be careful. Maybe I've changed forever. Maybe it's temporary. But I do know Vanessa's right. You're wild. And I don't want to change that. Free and easy, that's Pres Tilford. And I'm not much fun to be around now. I don't want to lose you because, for the time being, we're on different wavelengths. Nancy's party was too much for me."

"It wasn't the party. It was the company you kept. I should never have left you alone with Vanessa."

"But she was just being friendly. I'm confused, Pres."

"You're fine as long as you stay away from Vanessa Barlow," Pres said. "At least stay here long enough to enjoy my party. I know we'll convince you to stay. Don't make any decisions until after the party, okay?"

"Okay, Pres. But can we change it a little?"

"Sure. Your wish is my command." Pres meant what he said, but he was a little startled, and maybe a little hurt.

"I think the party had better be in the afternoon," she said. "Or better yet, a brunch. That is, if you want me to be at my best and really have a good time."

"But it would be more fun after the game. Then we can *really* celebrate."

"Is it a party for me, or for everybody else? I'm just telling you what I can handle."

"Is it what you do in the south, or something?"

Pres asked. Claudia seemed so determined to have a party that was less than the kind of party he had in mind, that he wondered if he was doing something wrong, something against the etiquette she was used to.

"No. There are parties after games. And parties before games. But I do love a brunch. It's so civilized."

"You want a civilized party?"

"That's exactly what I want. I've just had difficult surgery. I guess I'm more interested in beauty and peace than fireworks and rock music."

Pres felt his brain work overtime. Classical music, maybe even that string quartet Cleve Overmeyer had put together last year that had gone on to win the state's Junior Mozart competition. And croissants with fancy jams and marmalade. That was something his mother loved. Strawberries and peaches, too. His friends would die. This was absolutely not the kind of party he liked to go to, or give. It was too stuffy. "Like I said, Claudia, your wish is my command."

When he described for her what he had been conjuring up in his imagination, she said, "That's it exactly."

"Hey, everybody," Pres shouted to the five cheerleaders. They were gathering in their usual spot in the gym, near the door that led to the corridor where all the candy and soda machines were. "My party for Claudia's going to be a brunch. Don't make any plans for next Saturday

37

morning. And if you've got any already, cancel. Your presence is a must."

"A brunch?" Walt repeated.

"I think it's a great idea," Angie said. "We can party at Pres's before the game. And I'll have a party after."

"You guys can party all you want," Olivia said as she bent to touch her toes.

"What do you mean?" Walt asked. "You're coming, too, aren't you?"

"I'm climbing Winchester Peak this Saturday, remember?"

Pres hadn't thought of this complication. "I've planned it as a day party. I can't change my plans. You can climb Winchester Peak any time."

"I don't want to change my plans," Olivia said, "any more than you. As far as I'm concerned, I can party any time."

"But Ben and Patrick are sure to change their minds," said Pres. But when he looked at Mary Ellen, and then at Nancy, he got the distinct impression that he'd better not bet on their being any more reasonable than Olivia Evans.

Their cheerleading practice sessions over the next couple days became filled with something Mary Ellen couldn't put her finger on. Everyone seemed off in his own world.

"Okay," said Mary Ellen, when she could tell everyone had had just about enough. "Let's talk. We've got the game with Garrison in two days and we act as if we've got months to get our act together. With the party for Claudia we won't be able to practice Saturday morning."

"We need to," Walt said. "Maybe we should call off everything else." He was thinking of the climb.

"What?" Pres exclaimed. "I've worked my tail off putting together that party. It's *this* Saturday morning."

"I'm not sure we shouldn't do as Walt says," Nancy said. "We're starting to let other things get in the way. We have to figure out our priorities. And this squad should be first."

The conversation did not appeal at all to Pres. That was easy to see. He was beginning to get into one of his pacing bull moods.

Mary Ellen, aware of this, started to speak, but Olivia was quicker. "I'm climbing Saturday morning. And I'm not canceling it."

That cinched Mary Ellen's decision. She ordered a double practice for that afternoon and pre-game warm-ups ninety minutes earlier than usual on Saturday. Olivia was sure she'd have no problem with that.

Pres was thankful when that practice finally ended. He headed straight for the mall, mostly to blow off some steam. There was a great French fry place there, too, and that seemed exactly what his stomach craved.

It didn't take long, the way he was feeling, to finish a large order with gravy and manage a regular order, plain. As he was leaving he passed by Marnie's, where Mary Ellen modeled and where he knew a lot of the girls at school shopped. He would do just about anything for Mary Ellen now that she was going to try to change her work hours on Saturday to come to his party on time. Now that was a true friend. Everyone else on the squad seemed to be letting him down.

As he was thinking all this through, and trying to decide whether he should get a hamburger before heading home to the health food his mom served when his dad was out of town on business, he spotted Vanessa making her way through a rack of clothing near Marnie's front window. He cringed when they made eye contact. She waved and mouthed something. He certainly had better things to do than shoot the breeze with Vanessa Barlow. Then he saw the reason for her bright smile and excited manner.

Vanessa and Claudia were out shopping together. What a mistake. He made a beeline for her.

"Claudia! I thought you'd be at home." Pres was glad to see her shopping, but he certainly didn't want anything to happen that would lead to a setback. Doing too much or hearing the wrong thing from Vanessa would send her back to Virginia for sure.

Claudia's wideset, violet eyes sparkled at him. "Vanessa offered to take me shopping. We're getting ready for the party." She held up a soft white dress with a cowl neckline — cashmere, Pres figured. "How do you like it?"

"I love cashmere," he answered. Really, he

40

didn't know the first thing about women's fashions. "Try it on."

"Claudia's been telling me," Vanessa said, breaking into their conversation, "all about the doctor from California her mom wants to hire to watch over her this next month or so. He's some young, eligible intern. Isn't that how you described him, Claudia? Am I going to get to meet him at your party, Pres?"

"What doctor? Claudia didn't tell me about any doctor." He looked at Claudia, trying to keep his eyes from showing that he felt as if he'd just been stabbed.

"I told Mom I'd be fine," Claudia said. "But I guess she's feeling guilty about leaving me. I haven't agreed to it yet, so he's not even in town and won't be coming to the party. I told you that already, Vanessa. And Pres, he's just an intern."

"Just a young, eligible intern, that's all."

"Hey, you two, don't let me interfere or anything," Vanessa said. "But I do want to meet him. Who knows? Maybe I'll get interested in going to medical school, like Claudia here."

"Medical school?" Pres felt the world take off and spin out from under his feet.

"Oops." Vanessa covered her mouth, her eyes full of delight. "I guess I mentioned something I shouldn't. You two really should take some time to talk and get to know one another."

"Maybe you're right," Pres said. "Call me when you get done shopping," he said, moving toward the door.

41

"Pres!" Claudia shouted, but he was into the wide, boutique-lined corridor, out of earshot.

What do I have to compare with an intern? Pres thought. I'm just a high school senior, giving a silly party. A party for someone I love. And all he could do was hope that it all worked to keep Claudia in Tarenton.

CHAPTER 5

The five A.M. chill that filled the Evans home only served to fire Olivia's spirit as she stretched her arms into her long underwear. It fit tighter than a glove. She had to do well on the climb. She couldn't let the guys down or give them a reason to complain about having her along. That was why she was taking such care with her clothes, aiming for the perfect balance between warmth and ease of movement. Getting a chill up on Winchester Peak was a miserable thought, but so was feeling tight and weighted down with clothing.

In a moment of panic, she wondered if they were well enough organized for their climb. She hated forgetting something, but it had been hard to pin down Ben for a planning session. All they'd done was assign food to her. Thanks a bunch, she'd wanted to say, but she went along with their division of labor. First aid equipment had been assigned to Ben, and hiking gear and route-finding to Patrick. Patrick was appointed leader. Surely that was organized enough.

She looked at her alarm clock. Five-thirty. She'd better head downstairs. She didn't want Patrick honking that loud horn on his truck and waking up her parents. They didn't know a thing about the climb. She'd lied to them about an extra cheerleading practice before Pres's brunch, and they'd be expecting Walt to pick her up. They'd ask one question after another if they saw Patrick.

She stuffed herself with yogurt and sunflower seeds, a bowl of granola, and then most of a banana. She kept checking the front window as she ate. When Patrick arrived, he was fifteen minutes later than scheduled and Olivia was a bundle of nervous excitement.

Olivia grabbed her backpack, full of the kind of food she liked to have outdoors — gorp (a mixture of dried fruit, nuts, and M & M's), apples, cheese, crackers, chocolate, a thermos of coffee, all in quantities more than enough for three — plus some peanut butter and raspberry jam sandwiches. She quietly turned the doorknob and slipped out.

The sky was clear, still with a hint of deep, nighttime blue. It was warmer than she expected and she pulled off her wool cap and swung her hair free from the collar of her parka. Excitement shimmered in the air. She sucked in a big gulp of crisp air and smiled. It was great to be

44

alive. Already the climb was turning out to be exactly what she needed.

"What a great day," she said, greeting Patrick. "Where's Ben?"

"He wasn't ready. That's why I'm late. But he's coming. I guess he and Nancy stayed up for a while last night. We'll start about an hour later than we wanted, and that's always a poor way to begin a climb. I hope you don't mind."

"Mind? I'm so fired up for this climb, nothing's going to spoil it. I've been getting ready since five."

"I guess we could wish Ben had done the same."

"Yeah," she said. "I guess we could. I'm just glad he's still coming." Everyone at school would admire the venture a lot more because Ben was with them. Ben was a hero. Tarenton was lucky to have him as a transfer student, bringing them to victory in so many close basketball games. He'd go on to college on some basketball scholarship for sure, and be a big star there.

This time Ben was waiting for them and it didn't take even a horn honk to get him into the truck. Thirty minutes later they were headed down a dirt road, singing songs at the top of their lungs, intermittently replaying favorite scenes from Tarenton's closest basketball games and making predictions about that night's game against Garrison.

"Okay, this is it," Patrick announced, jerking the truck to a halt. He hopped out, gave a big yawn, and stretched his arms. "Fresh air. There's nothing like it." He headed toward the ranger station located at the base of Winchester Peak. "I'm going to register. I'll meet you at the back of the truck to unload in a few minutes."

Ben reached to help Olivia down from the truck. "I can make it by myself," she said.

Ben shook his head and smiled. "Pretty foolish of me, huh? You're going to climb this mountain with us, but you can't hop down from a truck without help." He walked away.

Oliva liked Ben Adamson. She hoped she'd have a chance to be with him in a new way on the mountain, a two-way street instead of just cheering him.

"Olivia!" Ben shouted. "Can we eat now?"

He was joking and she smiled. "How about some M & M's?" While Ben munched on handfuls of gorp, letting Olivia pick out the M & M's, Patrick returned.

"The rangers say the peak got dusted pretty good with snow yesterday," Patrick said. "What with the freeze last night and the warm weather that's been melting the snow lately, they're a little concerned about the possibility of an avalanche. They did some blasting this morning but nothing broke loose. They think it's pretty stable, but we should still be careful. They say the winter snow's pretty deep in some places and will be until there's been a good summer thaw."

"A little new snow really makes the peak look beautiful against the sky, though," Ben said.

"Yeah," Patrick agreed. "But new snow on top of old can make conditions dangerous and an

46

avalanche is serious business. If you guys want to back out, it's okay with me."

"Now," Ben said, "when was the last time there's been an avalanche set off by climbers? I don't remember ever even hearing about snowslides in this area. Mt. Heritage near Garrison is supposed to be dangerous that way during certain times of the year, but no one's ever been hurt."

"I think they happen all the time," Patrick said. "But you're right. I've never heard of anyone around here being in one."

"I'm not at all prepared for an avalanche," Olivia said. "I took my training in the summer. Are you sure they're right about avalanche possibilities?"

"One thing you get to know from meeting forest rangers who've worked in disasters like avalanches — believe every word they tell you. They think it's pretty stable, though. Especially if we stay on the windward side of the mountain. And that's the route we're headed up."

"You won't catch me going anywhere I'm not supposed to be," Olivia said. "Let's just be careful and do what the rangers said. I don't want to turn back now." The idea of an avalanche scared her, but since nothing had broken loose with blasting, she considered one a remote possibility.

"Me, either," Ben said. "Let's get going."

"It's majority rule, so we go," Patrick said.

"Oh, this is exciting," Olivia said. "More exciting than I ever dreamed. Walt would kill me if he knew what was going on."

"We can't tell anyone when we get back that we were even warned," Ben said. "I hate it when you're home, safe and sound, and everyone spoils things by saying you've done something stupid."

"Well," Patrick said, "we don't want to do anything stupid. Let's stop talking and get going."

"Yeah," Ben agreed.

The ground at the base as they started up the trail was moist, padded with pine needles, and Olivia found herself slipping slightly. She didn't want the guys to see and she grabbed a walking stick — a branch fallen from a lodgepole pine — for support.

"Good idea," Patrick said when he saw what she had done. He found a walking stick for himself, and that, together with his boots, wool plaid jacket, and backpack, made him look like a mountain man.

Olivia leaned with more force on her walking stick as the angle of their climb quickly steepened. Patches of deep, old snow began to appear, with a sprinkling of what must have been yesterday's dusting here and there. For the most part, the new snow looked as though it would soon melt. The rangers were right, though — the crusty layers of old snow wouldn't melt for quite a while.

In another hour, the sun and exertion combined to make Olivia and Patrick begin taking off the first layer of their clothing. Patrick discovered something that upset him very much. "I can't believe you didn't dress in layers, Adamson," he all but shouted at Ben. "You've got to do that up here. You can never predict what the weather will be like. If you sweat, and then the weather changes, you're done for."

"Keep cool," Ben said. He was wearing his red down parka, but with only a T-shirt underneath. "It's beautiful out. I was running late this morning and I didn't set out my gear last night. So, I sort of forgot some things. But you know me, I don't mind taking a few risks. Besides, I keep a pretty even temperature. I'm not in a sweat yet. I'll be fine."

"I brought an extra windbreaker," Olivia offered.

"And I've got another flannel shirt," Patrick said.

"Thanks," Ben said. "I'll be fine. Weather conditions couldn't be more perfect."

They continued on the hiking trail, making their way through trees, for about half an hour. The trees began to thin out then, signaling that timberline was approaching.

It didn't take long until they were upon an ominous block of gray granite. The technical stretch of their climb — what they were all looking forward to — was about to begin. From here on out it would be ropes and harnesses until they could start to scramble across boulders on their final ascent to the summit.

Everyone felt fine and they decided they'd tackle the rock face, rising above timberline with that portion of their climb, and forge their way to the peak, eating lunch on top. Once they made that decision, though, everyone got hungry.

"A few handfuls of gorp are all I need," Ben

said. "And I'm good for the hour or so it will take us to get up this rock face." He looked up at the hundred feet of gray rock they were going to scale, and then reached for the gorp Olivia had pulled from her pack.

Patrick began unwinding the rope from his pack, saying he'd better take an apple if Olivia thought she could spare one.

"I'm glad I know how Walt eats," Olivia said with a smile. She thought she had packed enough for six, but at the rate they were going they'd have nothing left once they returned to the bottom. She turned her face to the sun, now high overhead. It felt warm, even with the slight wind that had come up. There wasn't a cloud in the sky. The blue overhead had never seemed so clean to her, and she closed her eyes.

Everyone was probably arriving at Pres's brunch by now. She didn't want to check her watch to see the time. She wanted to feel free of that. And she really didn't want to concentrate on the others back in town. It would make her remember how rude she had been about Claudia's return. Her rudeness was so silly, so childish — all because she dreaded being reminded of sickness. This mountain, with its peace and beauty, made her feel she didn't have to struggle so hard to be separate from her past fight — and to be well.

"Olivia? Are you okay?" Patrick was shaking her shoulder. "You look dazed. Is it the altitude?"

"I'm okay. Really."

"We need to keep an eye on each other," he

said, as he unraveled the rope. "Really we do."

"Don't worry, Patrick," Ben said. "You worry too much."

"Well, I feel responsible."

"We're each responsible," Ben reminded him. "And that's how we're approaching this. If anything goes wrong, you're definitely not to blame."

"Nothing will go wrong," Olivia said. "I feel fine."

"If you get light-headed, tell us," Patrick ordered as he put on a climbing harness. "It's not a crime to rest." Patrick tied on to one end of the rope. With a rack of chocks he started up the sheer rock portion of Winchester Peak. They were clean climbing, not hammering in spikes that scarred the rock face, but using chocks that could be fitted into existing cracks and holes. Olivia, being more experienced than Ben, was the belay person on the ground, the one Patrick was tied to, as he climbed the one hundred foot rock face, setting in a chock every fifteen to twenty feet.

"I sure am glad we have Patrick leading the way," Ben said. "There's no one I trust more. He's a great guy."

"Yeah," Olivia agreed. She strained to watch Patrick maneuver his way slowly above them. "This is the hardest part, though. Waiting down here. I'd like a little action."

Suddenly, there was a thunderous roar. "What was that?" Ben shouted up to Patrick. "Can you see anything? It sounds like thunder."

A few rocks tumbled down around Olivia and Ben as Patrick, high above, looked around.

"Stay still," Olivia ordered. "We'll find out for ourselves."

"Was it an avalanche?" Ben asked with a shiver. "I've read they sound like that when they begin to roll. Maybe the rangers were right."

"Don't even talk about it," Olivia said. "We're not in avalanche country, really. These aren't the Rockies or the Sierras or some big mountain range like that."

Ben held out the palm of his right hand. "Rain," he said. "It was thunder. But I don't see a single cloud."

Olivia bent back and scanned the summit, straight up. Clouds had gathered high above. "It's just at the peak," she said. "It'll blow over. That kind of thing happens all the time."

The wind began to pick up, though, and grow suddenly chilly. The sun disappeared.

"Where did that storm come from?" Ben asked.

Olivia didn't bother to answer. It came from nowhere, just the way weather changes in the mountains always seemed to happen. There was a bright charge of lightning. And then a streak of sunshine. The air was charged with electricity. Olivia could smell it. "Maybe it will clear as quickly as it came up," she said. She hoped she was right.

Patrick signaled them that he was anchored at the top of the rock face.

"On belay?" Olivia asked.

"Belay on," Patrick shouted.

"Climbing," she called out.

"Climb," Patrick shouted. Back and forth they

went, as they had when Patrick had climbed, their words the proper signals for belaying. Olivia cleaned the route, pulling Patrick's chocks from the cracks, as she climbed.

She felt glorious, simply glorious, to be climbing, even in the rain that fell gently against her. The view of the valley below, when she took the time to look behind her, was breathtaking. The highway they had taken looked so miniscule.

The climb was strenuous and her legs, whenever she stopped, began to pump up and down uncontrollably. "Sewing machine" legs, they were called. To avoid that sensation, a strange mixture of pain and pleasure, she kept moving. Up, up she went. She felt like a spider. A spider with sore muscles. But she felt exhilarated once she was on top with Patrick. She hadn't remembered how great it felt once a stretch of technical climbing was an accomplished feat.

"Ben is cold. I can tell," she said, as soon as she had gotten to the edge where Patrick was anchored to a lone pine. "I'm worried about him."

"We'll stop and eat. And I think we ought to look for shelter. Boy, would some coffee taste good."

Ben seemed to have an awkward time making it up behind them. The rain intensified, cold and slashing. Patrick began to shout instructions and increase the tension on the climbing rope until it was taut between him and Ben. Patrick was practically pulling Ben up now.

"Damn," Patrick muttered.

"What's the matter now?"

"I smell snow."

"It isn't snowing," Olivia said.

"It isn't snowing *yet*," was Patrick's reply.

"Snow wasn't predicted," Olivia protested. But, sure enough, the sky surrounding the summit above was changing from dark storm clouds to the solid gray cloud cover that meant a snow storm was settling in. The wind, full of cold rain, lashed at Olivia's face and she strained to reach her hat in the pack on her back.

"Don't move," Patrick ordered. "Don't do anything until I have Ben up here."

Olivia did exactly as he said. They struggled to get Ben on solid ground, as he clambered over the last few feet of the rock face. He was drenched.

"Honest, guys," he said. "I know how to climb a lot better than that. I don't feel so good." His hands and lips were trembling the whole time they unroped him and got him out of his harness. "The flu's been going through my family. I bet that's it."

"It's not the flu," Patrick said. "We've got to get you warm." He took a moment to look at their surroundings. The mountain now went up at a manageable incline. It was beginning to sleet, the wind whipping and slashing fragments of watery ice. Visibility was poor. Patrick ran his right hand over his face and slung away a layer of cold water. "Let's find cover and get something to eat. Maybe this miserable storm will pass."

Patrick bent over, carefully leading the way up the mountain. They trudged their way to a sloping field. They were above timberline now, and there wasn't more than a single, scraggly pine to be seen. And there was snow — old, crusty snow — that broke underfoot as they struggled forward. With each step they sank about a foot. Suddenly, Patrick was in snow almost up to his waist.

"This is like a nightmare," Patrick said.

"Don't say that," Olivia ordered in a hoarse whisper. Ben was shivering violently behind her. "If you can get out of the snow without us, I want to head over to those rocks." She nodded toward an outcropping of boulders. "At least they'd protect us from the wind."

"Good idea," was all Patrick said. He let her head out a good distance before he began struggling to the surface. When Olivia turned to look back at him he yelled, "Keep going!"

Once again there was a thunderous roar as a sheet of ice broke away below Patrick and headed down the mountain at breakneck speed. Patrick, spread-eagled on the snow, clung for dear life. "It's not as bad as it looks," he said, almost in a whisper, to Ben and Olivia, stopped dead in their scrambling crawl toward the rock outcropping. He motioned them on, beginning his own careful, crablike crawl.

When he got to Olivia and Ben, they were leaning so tightly against the rocks and staying so still that they seemed glued in place. "I don't feel like moving," Olivia said, breathless. "Ever again."

"Well," Patrick said, "this isn't much cover. We probably should keep going till we find something better."

"I'm too cold to move," Ben said, shivering.

"It's warm against the rock, and it cuts the wind. I want to stay," Olivia said. She felt frightened, truly frightened. She couldn't at all figure out how they'd ever manage to get down under these conditions. The weather simply had to change. Everyone always said it could change quickly in the mountains. If you don't like the weather, wait a minute and it will change. That was the standard description of mountain weather.

"Let's pass around that thermos of coffee," Patrick said. The three of them were huddled together, sheltered only slightly by the wall of rock. "Give it to Ben first. And we'll decide what to do next. If only we'd brought overnight camping gear. A sleeping bag is all we need."

"We'd need three," Olivia said, handing the thermos to Ben but keeping her grip on it, too, just in case he lost hold. "We each should have taken care of ourselves better."

"We sure should have," Patrick said. "But a single bag would help. A good instructor once told me the best protection against exposure is for two people to get inside a sleeping bag and keep each other warm."

"Really," Olivia said, slightly startled by the idea. "That would sure start rumors back at school."

"Rumors don't really matter, do they? Not when it's a matter of life and death." Patrick stared off in the vast space in front of them that suddenly filled with blowing, almost blinding snow. "Damn," he muttered. "I knew we were in for snow. I just never thought it would be this much."

Olivia snuggled tightly against Ben. "Get to his other side," she told Patrick. "He needs cover more than either of us."

Patrick crept carefully in front of them to Ben's other side. Instantly, Olivia felt a chill where Patrick had been huddled against her. And in that instant she realized she would do just about anything to survive.

CHAPTER 6

All Nancy could think of, from the moment she woke up Saturday morning, was Ben and what he was doing. She lay in bed for quite a while, in her mind watching him get ready for the climb, yawning and stretching and having a hard time waking up, then scrambling to get dressed. He'd be the hero on the mountain, full of vigor and determination, though it always seemed to take him extra long to wake up. It seemed to her that he did everything with abandon, including sleep. But once he was awake — watch out.

Abandon. That word rolling through her sleepy head had a luscious feel to it, reminding her of Ben's good-night kisses the night before.

She headed for the shower, first checking the weather outside. The air looked wonderfully crisp, full of sparkling sun. She was happy for the climbers.

Oh, well, let them get sore thigh muscles, Nancy thought as she reached for her bathrobe and went into the bathroom. Me? I'm on my way to the easy pleasures of a great brunch. She was very glad to have something to do. Time would pass quickly, and she'd be with Ben in no time.

Walt picked her up in his Jeep. Mary Ellen was in the backseat, studying herself in a hand mirror, and the next stop was Angie's.

"You look great," Walt greeted Nancy. "I'm going to end up with quite a bevy of beauties."

Mary Ellen looked beautiful, as usual, in a silky white dress with deep green Oriental-style brush strokes and a white wool coat. "Where'd you get that coat, Mary Ellen? It's gorgeous."

"I know," she said, her face lit up with a big smile. "It's an end-of-season sale item at Marnie's. When I couldn't get to the store this morning, and I explained why, they thought up this idea of wearing some of Marnie's clothes at the party. I'm not technically modeling, and don't breathe a word to anyone, please, that I don't own these clothes. I'm just to say where I got the dress and coat, if anyone asks. In fact, I think they'll probably give me both, at least at a good discount, for doing this."

"That's great. The coat's stunning."

"I really like white coats, too," Mary Ellen agreed. "It's funny. You'd think they'd remind me of snow and cold. "

"Reminds me of bunnies," Walt said. "Soft and warm."

"I sure miss Ben," Nancy moaned.

59

"Not me," Walt said. "I haven't thought about him in days."

Nancy smiled. She was glad to be going to Pres's party with Walt and the rest of the squad. They talked about what to expect at the party, and how glorious it must be to be headed up Winchester Peak on such a lovely day. It seemed in no time they'd picked up Angie and were at the Tilfords' front door being greeted by the Tilford maid.

"The receiving line's in the library," she told them.

They looked at each other. "Receiving line?" they remarked in unison.

"I think a receiving line must be a southern custom, or something," Angie whispered as they headed through the large, two-story foyer.

"Wait till some of the guys get here," Mary Ellen said. "They'll have a field day with *that* custom. Pres will never hear the end of it."

They greeted Pres and Claudia. "Boy, am I glad you guys are the first to get here," Pres said. "What do you think about a receiving line? My mother came up with the idea to make sure everyone got a chance to welcome Claudia. I figured she'd know about this kind of stuff, but now that we've tried to stand here like a receiving line I'm not so sure."

While Walt and Angie and Nancy tried to help Pres out, Mary Ellen looked around. Claudia and Pres seemed to fit naturally in a place as elegant as the Tilford mansion. They were at ease. She could hear Claudia say she did like the graciousness of a receiving line but it didn't seem right for their get-together. She'd probably been in plenty already, Mary Ellen figured. Parties at country clubs, debutante affairs that Mary Ellen had only read about. That was the kind of life Claudia Randall had already led, and the kind of life she was guaranteed if she stuck with Pres Tilford.

Some people have all the luck, thought Mary Ellen, realizing that no matter how successful she became with her modeling, she'd never redo her past. She'd never have what Pres and Claudia had — the confidence that being born with money gave one. It was a powerful sort of comfort and security, something Mary Ellen figured earning money later in life really couldn't buy.

The door bell rang again and again, and Mary Ellen watched people being greeted. Someday she'd have a penthouse overlooking Central Park. Would there be a man in her life? In her mind's eye she stood and gazed at her penthouse apartment, lined with windows that offered a breathtaking view of the city. But she couldn't tell if there was room for a man in those stylish rooms.

"I wonder how the climb is going," Nancy said, catching up with Mary Ellen just as she approached the greenhouse doors. "From what I hear, they're sure going to miss some great food." Nancy shivered. "Boy, it's drafty in here. I've even got goose bumps." She rubbed her arms.

Suddenly it seemed the entry behind them was flooded with members of the basketball team.

"Hey, hey, hey," Harry Mathias said loudly, his eyes scanning the rich surroundings. "Reception line! Who cares? Where's the food?"

"Don't leave any fingerprints on the silver," Jake Dixon called out.

There was laughter, and some other joke that Mary Ellen didn't hear. "Hey, a swimming pool!" Bob Ryder called out. "And there's a table set up outside. What does Pres think this is? Summer? I'm not going out there. It's going to snow."

"Snow?" Nancy said. "It can't snow." She shivered from head to foot. "I can't stand thinking about how cold Winchester Peak must be if I'm chilly down here, and in a house to boot. I sure hope they see snow coming and turn around."

"Snow isn't in the forecast," Mary Ellen assured her. "And those three? If anyone's prepared for all eventualities, it's them. Patrick's rescued me from more calamities. . . ." Even as she spoke, Mary Ellen knew she was saying the wrong thing. Patrick had the capacity to rescue anybody and everybody. But if he was in trouble, who would rescue him? "Come on, let's go enjoy the party and get away from the greenhouse. That's got to be where this draft is coming from."

Just as Mary Ellen and Nancy got to the library doors the doorbell rang and a fist began to pound on the door. "Let us in. Hurry, let us in."

Mary Ellen would recognize that pleading voice anywhere. "Vanessa," she said to Nancy. "Do you think we could manage to turn the lock on the door and keep her in whatever torture she's enduring?"

"It's the cold," Nancy sighed. Suddenly she thought of how the weatherman always gave a separate report for the mountains and that it was always thirty, even forty, degrees colder there.

The door burst open, letting in Vanessa and Nat and cold, blowing rain. Vanessa immediately shook raindrops from her red cashmere dress.

"Poor Ben," Nat said as soon as he saw Nancy. "I sure wouldn't want to be him right now. They must be a good three to four hours into their climb and now this weather comes up."

"Poor Ben," Vanessa mocked. "And poor everybody else." She walked straight ahead, shaking her hair so that drops of water splattered across Mary Ellen's face.

Mary Ellen sputtered, but then caught her breath. Vanessa was wearing the same dress as Claudia, only in red, not white. She was sure of it. What Vanessa wouldn't do for the excitement of a little ill will.

"Oh, boy," Mary Ellen muttered. "We'll have fireworks in no time that'll warm this place like the Fourth of July." Mary Ellen recognized the dress, of course, from Marnie's. And Vanessa looked a hundred times better in the dress than Claudia had, so much so that Mary Ellen hadn't really commented on how Claudia looked when she greeted her. White was not Claudia's color, at least not right now after surgery. And the style, cut so smoothly at the waist line, was not flattering to a figure other than the kind Vanessa had. Claudia was far too thin right now. Didn't anyone at the store help Claudia with her choice?

63

But then, it was apparent, from the way that Vanessa marched right up to Claudia and Pres, that Claudia had had help all right. Vanessa's help.

"Hey, Pres," Harry suddenly shouted. "It's starting to snow. Looks like a regular blizzard building up outside. Can I build a fire?"

"Sure," Pres said without turning his steely-eyed gaze from Vanessa who was standing directly in front of him, daring a comment. "It looks like people do whatever they damn well please around here."

Claudia, with more poise than Mary Ellen had ever seen from anyone, reached out her right hand. "Vanessa, you look stunning." It was easy to tell she meant it, too.

Vanessa seemed to grow sheepish right before everyone's eyes, shrinking an inch or two, completely taken aback by Claudia's gentle poise. For a few seconds she seemed genuinely confused. Then she rallied and completely ignoring Claudia's outstretched hand, she headed for the food.

"What nerve," Pres sputtered. "She's such a spider."

"It's still my party. Vanessa can't spoil it, Pres, honey. I plan to enjoy every minute of it. And I'm having a great time, really." Claudia kissed his cheek and tugged at his hand. "Let's go listen to the music. And then see if Celia needs help in the kitchen. My stomach's absolutely rumbling."

"Well, sure," Pres said. He looked around the room. "Everyone's here who's coming, I guess." There were about forty friends in the library and another fifteen or so wandering around the first floor.

Mary Ellen swallowed hard watching Pres walk out, his arm around Claudia. Claudia had strength, and courage. Mary Ellen hadn't remembered thinking of her that way before she went into the hospital. She'd changed somehow, in a subtle way. She was softer. Pres was lucky to be with her, she decided.

"Food's coming!" It was Walt, looking as though he was walking on air in his excitement about the approach of food. He headed toward Mary Ellen. "It looks terrific. I've been out in the kitchen, helping. Celia thinks I'd make a great cook." He was munching on what looked like some kind of miniature brown sugar and cinnamon bun.

"How can you be interested in food at a time like this?" Nancy asked. She cradled a mug of hot black coffee in her hands and let the steam rise to warm her face. "It's snowing down here. For all we know the three of them are trapped on Winchester in a blizzard."

"It's really only a light snow," Walt said. "It could be a bright, sunny day up on the mountain. The weather changes there so quickly, and it's never like it is down here. You worry too much, Nancy. Flurries like this come up suddenly and blow away just as quickly this time of year. Besides, they've got brains. I bet they're headed for the truck right now. Or in it already."

Mary Ellen didn't like to think about danger, but she knew no one was safe, really, from accidents. Anything could happen, like the car accident she'd been in. "Don't worry," she told Nancy. "Walt's right. It could be nice as a spring day up there."

"Well," Walt said, looking at the small bits of fast falling snow that were hitting the tall library windows, melting rapidly and streaming to the sill, "if it makes you feel any better, I'm worried. But it's time to eat. Try to take your mind off them and enjoy yourself. We can't do anything for them here."

"I thought this was going to be a nice day," Pres announced to the group that was gathering to devour everything in sight. He majestically set down the large silver tray of shrimp he had been carrying. "But it's a blizzard out there. You don't mind if things are less than perfect, do you, Claudia?"

Claudia put her arm around Pres. "You make everything perfect," she said as she snuggled close to him.

"This party is stupid," Nancy muttered to Mary Ellen and Walt. "We've got a fire to keep us warm. What about out on that mountain?"

CHAPTER

7

Ben was trying everything he could to stay warm. He couldn't let Patrick and Olivia know how miserable he felt. They'd only say it was his own fault. There were two things in life he hated: being criticized, especially for doing things the quick and easy way; and being treated like a baby. He hopped up and down, threw his arms again and again around his chest in a big bear hug, and pulled his clothing over places it was never meant to be. "Man," he finally sputtered. "There's just no way around it. It's getting colder."

Patrick was scared by all his responsibility now that weather conditions had changed for the worse. Sure, he knew pretty much what to do, and was confident that the others hadn't been wrong in picking him as leader. He was the most skilled, which right now maybe wasn't saying much. He wished Olivia and Ben were more experienced. They had enough skill to climb Winchester Peak. But knowledge of technical climbing wasn't what would get them home safe and sound. The problem, as he saw it, was that they lacked a certain kind of experience that came from hours and hours of climbing and seeing just what kind of power and danger the outdoors was capable of unleashing. He felt alone. "I hate to head back down with it snowing like this. We're not in the best of shape anymore." Another fifteen minutes in these blizzard conditions, though, and Patrick knew he'd have to order a descent. A very careful descent. It would be easy to get lost.

"Look at this, will you?" Olivia said, holding up her dirty wool mitten for inspection. Three M & M's — a yellow, a red, and a brown — were hanging, one by one, from the fuzz. "Frozen to my mitten. I've always loved frozen M & M's. But in the right place." She smiled and got what she wanted, smiles from the two boys.

Patrick started to pace back and forth, while Olivia and Ben huddled together. Olivia could feel Ben's breath against her cheek. She could tell, from the way he was shivering now, that he wouldn't be able to take much more. Not sitting like this, anyway. They had to get moving. "We ought to move, Patrick. We could get down by nightfall, couldn't we, if we started now?"

"We won't be able to do even *that* if this snow keeps up. Damn!" He motioned for Olivia to move over and he took the seat that blocked the almost gale-force wind that whipped the mountain, blowing snow around in a blinding, hypnotizing fashion. "But you're right. There's no way we can wait this out and be alive to tell about it."

"I figured," Olivia said quietly. "I'm scared, Patrick."

"I'm scared, too," he admitted. "I don't think that's an unreasonable feeling with what we're facing. We're ending up with a lot more difficult climb than we ever set out to make. But things like this happen. It will be a good experience to have under your belt." He was trying to make them feel more confident. If they were going to head back, they would need to do it with confidence.

"Well," Ben said. "I can't afford to be scared. I've got a game tonight. There's no way I'm letting a little snow keep me away from that game. Let's head out. I feel warmer just thinking about getting back down to the bottom."

"Take it easy," Patrick told him. "Everything's different from before. There's at least a foot of snow covering everything. It clings in funny ways, Ben. We have to go down carefully. So just take it easy. Please. Visibility's really lousy, too, and that has to make the going slow. I'm going to do the best I can to get you both to the game."

"You're the leader," Ben said, steadying Olivia as she stood for the first time in nearly an hour.

Patrick explained that they could avoid the steep rock face they had ascended if they headed a little further west of their route up the mountain. The forest ranger had told him about that, and he'd sighted that particular route from the base, catching a glimpse of it once in a while as they climbed. "It's not as difficult, but we still have to be careful."

Ben sighed heavily. "I know you're the leader and all, but if we're too careful we'll *never* get down. I say we've got to get down fast."

Olivia turned to him. "You take it easy, Ben," she said. "I went on this climb for excitement and we've got plenty here, to say the least. More than I ever bargained for. Patrick's right about being careful. And if you don't think this is dangerous, then you don't know what's happening."

"Okay, okay. So it's dangerous. I'll take it easy. It'll make for a good story one way or the other. But you don't have to get on my case. We're part of a team, remember?"

"I'm sorry," she said, meaning to apologize for her brusqueness but not for what she had said. She meant every word of it. "I guess I'm getting tense." She tried to rub away the flakes of snow clinging to her eyelashes, but only ended up scratching her face with her icy mittens.

"Don't worry about it," Ben said. "I'm a little tense, too. Maybe I just show my fear differently."

Olivia nodded. She kissed his cheek. "See you at the bottom. And at the game."

Ben winked at her. "Yeah, tiger. See ya at the game. It'll be an easy win."

Getting moving lifted their spirits. Patrick in the lead, Olivia in the middle, Ben bringing up the rear, they were unroped, having decided they weren't going to try any technical moves or get too close to any exposed sheer drops in this kind of blizzard. They moved slowly, almost shuffling along. Every once in a while Patrick would take out his compass and check their position.

"What's up?" Ben shouted. He had gotten even further behind and really had to shout. It was almost hard to see him through the whirling, large flakes of snow. "We aren't lost, are we?"

"Ssh!" Patrick hissed at him, motioning for silence with his hand.

The mountain rumbled above them. Snow was breaking away someplace. Olivia looked down at her boots. Little rivulets of snow trickled down the mountain right where she was standing. "Is it coming our way?" she asked Patrick. They were back among the pines, but she knew being in the trees was no guarantee of not being threatened by the danger of an avalanche.

"No," he said slowly, more engaged in listening than talking. "I don't think so." He cocked his head. "It sounds like it's on the other side, just like the rangers predicted. But I sure don't like it."

At the same instant, they both turned back toward Ben. For some reason he was moving away from them, more in the direction of the rumbling snow. In a flash Patrick headed at top speed toward Ben, stumbling and thrashing his way through the sparse scattering of lodgepole pine. The way he moved, like a bear gone mad, scared her.

Olivia felt her heart pound loud and fast. She took off after Patrick, looking beyond him to see what Ben was up to. Ben turned toward them and waved, motioning for them to join him as he headed out onto a snowy ledge.

Suddenly Ben vanished. There was a wisp of snow, and he was gone, disappearing into the snowy chasm beyond.

Olivia let go a sound she didn't know she was capable of making, a terrible sound that came from her belly and heart and head and exploded from her. She plunged ahead through the snow, falling, scraping her face against a branch, her knee against exposed rock. She stumbled on. Suddenly she hit the ground.

"Olivia," Patrick said hoarsely as he tackled her at the knees. "You can't go any closer."

"Where is he?" Snow burned her chin. Rubbing it off with her ice-packed mitten only made it worse.

"We've got to crawl to the edge. He just went down. God knows what kind of a fall he took."

"The ledge will take my weight better than yours," she said, spitting snow from her mouth. She did not like being tackled. It was frightening hitting the ground like that, but she knew Patrick had only tried to protect her. As he released his hold and let her crawl forward by inches, she could feel his fingers at her ankles, ready to grab if she started to fall or slip.

What had just happened couldn't have happened. That's what she felt. As if this were some nightmare, and a scream would wake her up. Oh, God, please let Ben be all right. Make him be standing a few feet below and smiling up, as if it were some big joke. Let it be one of those stunts he sometimes pulls. I'll forgive him, I promise.

She dragged herself to the very edge. Exactly at the moment she came to a halt, Patrick took an even more firm hold of her ankles. She gasped the moment she saw Ben's body sprawled on the snow a good hundred feet below.

"He isn't moving, Patrick. And I think he had to hit a bunch of rock halfway down. Oh, God, he's more than a hundred feet away."

Patrick began pulling her back through the snow from the edge. "You stay back. Let me get a look."

Patrick worked furiously to get his climbing harness on and anchor the rope to a tree. He positioned Olivia so she could belay him. "Do you understand?" he asked, talking slowly to her as if she were deaf. "I'm roped to you. I need you right now, Olivia. *Ben* needs you. We have to figure out what to do."

She nodded to let him know she understood, and braced her heels against the ground. "I'm okay. We've got to get down to him."

"That's what I'm going to figure out how to do. Are you okay?" he asked for what seemed to Olivia like the thousandth time.

"Yeah. Hurry up." She felt all right because she had to. That was climbing. Always a matter of life and death. No room for indulgence. She could cry, but only if it didn't interfere. She began to shiver. Her mind went blank.

"Come on," Patrick said, standing suddenly above her. "I see a way down. I don't want to get into anything too difficult. Not with just the two of us, and not in these conditions. It may take a while, but a roundabout way will be safer."

Olivia felt as if she were in a daze. "Coffee," she said. "I need coffee first."

"Good idea," Patrick said. He brushed away a good half inch of snow that seemed to have collected almost instantaneously on the sleeve of his jacket. It was a heavy, wet snow. "I've got to come up with a plan."

"I'll stay with Ben when we reach him," she said.

Patrick bit his lip and lowered his eyes. "I don't think anybody's going to need to stay with Ben."

She really already knew that. "We have to make sure."

"I know we do."

Olivia looked away. "Let's get started."

It would take them nearly an hour to get to Ben. It couldn't be more than two, maybe three, hours before it would be nightfall. What would they do then?

Patrick was angry at Ben. He had never felt so angry at anybody in his life. The guy knew better. Why'd he always have to be such an adventurer? Why couldn't he just stay still? Damn! Ben couldn't be dead. Not Ben, Patrick kept repeating to himself. Damn!

He led the way, poking at snow as they inched downhill, fearful that there might be a false edge built by the new snow that would collapse with their weight, fearful of another slip — just what must have happened to Ben.

What exactly had happened? Patrick kept going over in his mind the last minutes he had seen Ben. Shouldn't he have noticed Ben was too close to the edge? What did the guy think he was doing? He must have been watching the avalanche.

What exactly do I think I'm doing? Patrick asked himself. What kind of a leader am I? I was supposed to be picking the trail, watching out for everybody. Wasn't I paying enough attention? Why didn't I holler for him to catch up with us? What was I doing the moment Ben inched too close to the edge? Where was I?

"Do you see him yet?" Olivia asked. "Are we going the right way?"

"Of course we're going the right way." He almost exploded at her. He wanted to kick something. But his responsibility brought him up short. No. Olivia was right to question him. They weren't going the right way. They were headed too far downhill.

It didn't take but a second for Patrick to angle them off to the left just a little bit. And there Ben was. Only parts of his red down parka were visible through the snow that had accumulated.

"Don't run!" Olivia shouted.

Patrick halted. She's right. I've got to be careful. "Right," he said, more to himself than her. Ben had fallen onto a narrow ledge, no more than eight feet wide, and they had no idea how strong that was. There was an outcropping of rock fifty feet up, midway between the ledge they were on now and where Ben had been standing. There was no way, in his fall, that he could have missed hitting that.

Ben lay on his stomach, facedown. Patrick knelt beside him and brushed away the snow around his head. In his mind he reviewed all he'd ever learned about first aid. In life-threatening emergencies, deal with the ABC's: airway, breathing, and circulation. Check pulmonary resuscitation, cardio-pulmonary resuscitation, and then control of hemorrhage and shock, his mind mechanically fed back. There were a few bruises on Ben's right cheek that Patrick could see had bled slightly. "He broke his neck," he told Olivia. "He's dead."

"Check," she said, numbly.

"Check what?"

"Check his heart. His pulse. Make sure he isn't breathing."

"He's dead."

"Damn it, check!" she ordered. "He isn't dead until I see he's not breathing."

Patrick was careful when he turned Ben over. He really didn't want to turn him, just as he wouldn't have wanted to move anyone for whom movement might mean certain death. "Listen for yourself."

Olivia bent over him, gently, taking off her hat so her ears were uncovered. Her hair fell on Ben and she kissed him. She was crying.

"We've got to get going, Olivia," Patrick said, reaching out for her hand. "Maybe, if we head toward the east side, we'll make it down. It's the fastest way."

"But that's the avalanche chute the rangers warned us about."

"Yeah, but it's the fastest, easiest way. We don't have the strength to do anything else."

"You go, then. I can't leave him. Not here, not in the cold."

"He can't feel the cold, Olivia." What he said hit him in a funny way. He began to cry, sobs breaking from his throat, but no teardrops falling.

Olivia reached out her arms. Tears were streaming down her cheeks.

Patrick leaned against her. He didn't know what he'd do without her. He needed comfort, the last thing he ever thought he'd need on a mountain climb.

For a while they sat. The snow fell around them, and on Ben, lightly covering his face and hair. Finally, Patrick pulled out his extra flannel shirt and covered Ben's face. Ben didn't look peaceful, exactly, but he didn't look afraid, either. He was somewhere where earthly feelings had no meaning, anyway.

"It's time to go, Olivia." He said this firmly, but as gently as he felt he could and make her see that, for their own safety, they had to leave.

"I know," she said. "Nothing will ever be the same."

"We'll be back for him."

CHAPTER

8

When Olivia, Patrick, and Ben did not show up at Pres's party as promised, Walt followed the alternate plan he and Olivia had devised. He called Mrs. Evans, explained Olivia had forgotten her uniform for the game, and that he'd be stopping by to pick it up for her.

"That girl," Mrs. Evans had said. "Someday she'll forget something really important."

Walt didn't know what to say so he just said, "Right," and hung up. Olivia and her mom had very different ideas about what was important. And compared to him, Olivia never forgot anything, never left a single detail to chance. She was the one who had realized it was possible she might get back from the climb with only enough time to get ready for the game, and had concocted their plan. In the event they were later than they expected, she'd meet Walt at the gym.

Walt was glad to have something to do before

their pre-game warm-ups, even if it meant coming in contact with Mrs. Evans, not one of his favorite people. Something, anything, that occupied all his anxious energy. Otherwise he'd worry about Olivia even more, as he was sure Nancy was worrying right now about Ben. The snow falling during the party had made Nancy frantic, and she had hardly said a word when Walt took her, Mary Ellen, and Angie home. It didn't make any difference to her that Walt could demonstrate, with his handling of his Jeep, that conditions really weren't all that dangerous.

But Walt knew they *were* dangerous, even as he tried to convince Nancy of just the opposite. An unexpected storm always gave reason for concern.

As he dressed for the game, pulling on his white wool cheerleading sweater and slim red pants and then combing back his hair, Walt kept sight through his window of the snow softly falling through the evergreens in the forest around his home. The snow had let up some. But what was frightening was that it would soon be dark.

He was getting more and more anxious and he didn't know what to do about it. He wanted to call each of the cheerleaders, just in case they'd gotten word, but he didn't do that. He'd acted so certain at the party that everything was okay, he couldn't show his alarm now.

Everything's okay, he told himself. Everything's okay. But he called Nancy just in case she'd heard anything. Before he even asked, though, he could tell she hadn't, so he said, "I'll pick you up if you like. I have to pick up Olivia's uniform so I'll be in your neck of the woods."

That seemed to relieve her. And Walt felt better, too. Everything's okay, he said, starting to pace. He looked at the clock. Only five.

He headed for his Jeep. Being outside would help. Maybe he'd spot Patrick's truck and be the first to celebrate their arrival. "If this is your idea of excitement, Olivia Evans," he muttered as he slammed the Jeep door, sending inches of snow flying, "I've had more than I can take. I hope you have, too."

As soon as they got to the gym Nancy sat down on the floor and tucked herself into a ball.

"What's wrong with Nancy?" asked Mrs. Engborg, the cheerleading squad's coach, a dynamic woman who seemed invigorated by the snowfall.

"She's waiting for Ben," explained Walt as he paced the strip of cement that ran along the edge of the gym floor.

"I thought you were going to run through your new routine," Mrs. Engborg said. "That's why I'm here early. We're lucky with the storm. Hardly anyone's here yet and we'll be able to keep the routine a surprise. It's really a great cheer, Walt. You and Olivia are to be congratulated."

"Thanks," was all he said. "I'll tell Olivia you said so when she gets here."

"She isn't here? But I saw Mary Ellen and Angie in the locker room. I thought she was with them."

81

Nancy listened without moving from her hunched-over position as Walt explained that Olivia had left early in the morning, with Patrick and Ben, to climb Winchester Peak. "As far as any of us knows, they're still not back," Walt added.

"Climbing?" Mrs. Engborg drew in a deep breath and seemed to hold it while she thought about the news. "I don't like that at all. Why didn't someone tell me? There's a lot to be aware of if you're going to go climbing at this time of year. Storms like this. . . ." She didn't complete her thought. She didn't have to. Concern was written all over her face. "Let me go get the girls. We've got to get started. We simply can't afford to keep waiting."

Carefully shaking snow off his jacket, Pres joined Walt, standing by the water fountain. "Sorry I'm late. The traffic over by Dr. Harroldson's is really lousy. There are accidents all over the place." He ran his fingers through his snow-drenched hair. "The parking lot's still pretty empty. If we want to have a good warm-up session, and not give away all our secrets, we'd better get started."

Nancy felt she wouldn't — couldn't — move. She sat with her knees against her chest, her chin resting on her knees, her eyes sometimes staring at the empty gym, sometimes at the floor. She didn't want to do anything until she heard the news that Ben was safe. She was controlling all she felt — the fear that they were huddled into a ball together out on the mountain or wedged in Patrick's truck in a ditch, injured and cold. She couldn't move. She had to stay like this just to survive. All she wanted was for Ben to walk into the gym in the next minute. He *had* to.

"Okay," Mrs. Engborg ordered. "We're ten minutes later getting started for pre-game warm-ups than we planned. Let's get going. I know you're all worried, but exercise and thinking about something else will help. Come on, Nancy. You've got to move."

"Without Olivia?" Walt asked.

"Without Olivia. We've got to figure out what to do in case she doesn't show in time for the game. Why didn't any of you tell me about the climb?" In return for her question she got sheep-ish stares. "Okay, okay. It doesn't matter. Let's just get started. Mary Ellen, put your squad into action. We don't have a minute to lose."

Mary Ellen gave instructions to her squad. Her eyes constantly swept the bleachers, expect-ing to see Patrick give her his usual big wave. Maybe something *had* happened to them. Maybe they were in a hospital.

"Stop, everybody," Mary Ellen ordered just as they'd finished their usual stretches, at half the normal pace, and the synchronized leg lifts that were part of one of the routines Angie had composed. "We can't go on."

Mrs. Engborg rose from her seat in the first row of bleachers. "The breakdancing routine that Walt wrote," she said. "I want to see that."

"But we can't," pleaded Mary Ellen. She could feel the effect she was having on her squad. Nancy stood with her mouth open, as if she was going to be sick. Walt looked away and Mary Ellen wondered if he was fighting back tears. She was sorry to upset her squad, but she was frightened. Nothing bad happened to Patrick, ever. But she used to think that about herself, and then she'd had the car wreck that taught her that anything could happen. "Something's happened. I think we should check the hospitals."

"You have to go on," Mrs. Engborg said. "We'll be notified if anything's happened. If you want, I'll call the hospitals once the game starts. But you must go on. That's why I picked each and every one of you." She looked into the faces of her squad, one by one. "I knew I could count on you, whatever happened, win or lose, through personal problems or with life a big bowl of cherries. Olivia would want you to go on. You don't think the team's going to call off the game because Ben's not here, do you?"

"I think calling the hospitals is a great idea," Walt said, ignoring the point Mrs. Engborg was trying to make. "We have to do *something*. I'd be all for the teams calling quits on the game and starting a search party. How can we cheer and shoot baskets when the three of them are missing?"

That only made Nancy start to sob. Angie reached out and put her arms around Nancy's shoulders. "It'll be okay, Nancy. Really it will."

Mrs. Engborg, looking truly concerned, handed Nancy a Kleenex. Nancy twisted it between her fingers and seemed to hold her breath to stop her crying. "I guess you all think I'm

84

just being a baby about all this," Nancy sobbed.

"No," Pres said. "It's okay to cry. That doesn't make you a baby. But we need you now. I feel like cheering."

"We know *you* feel like cheering," Nancy said, finally using the Kleenex Mrs. Engborg had handed her and blowing her red nose. "Claudia's home safe and sound."

"That's true," Pres said. "But it's more than that. I feel like cheering for them — Patrick, Olivia, and Ben. Out there on the mountain, or in the truck, or wherever they are."

Angie said, stroking Nancy's dark hair, damp with tears, "We could cheer for them with all our hearts."

"I like the idea," Walt said thoughtfully. "If I thought I was cheering for Olivia, then I'd be able to concentrate."

"It's a good idea, Pres," Mary Ellen said. "Let's do it. But I still want the hospitals called. I won't be able to concentrate unless I know something's being done."

"Please, Mrs. Engborg," Nancy pleaded.

"I said I'd call and I will. Now, let's get something started here to make up for Olivia's being gone. I know we can't replace her, but. . . ."

"We know what you mean, Mrs. Engborg," Walt said. "The show must go on. Olivia would want it that way."

"Where's Ben, Nancy?" Nat asked, running up to the squad just as they were beginning to get organized for warm-ups. "He's not still on that climb, is he?"

"He is," Nancy said. "They meant to be back, and something must have happened."

"I'm sure Ben will show," Nat said. "We won't win without him."

Mary Ellen leaped into a handstand, from there going into a solo breakdance routine while the couples did an updated version of the jitterbug. Then they formed a pyramid, Olivia's absence from the top seeming only to make them tougher and more determined.

> "Roar for more!
> Raise that score!
> Send old Garrison out the door!"

Pres's idea pulled them together, enabling them to concentrate by giving them a reason to go on, and Mrs. Engborg applauded as she never had. Of course, Mary Ellen knew their concentration could fall apart any time. They were getting their act together barely enough to get through pregame warm-ups.

CHAPTER

Olivia didn't care if she ever got home. She'd never tell Patrick that, not as serious as he was being getting them back down the mountain now. But she just didn't care. She didn't care if she lived or died. What did it matter after what had happened to Ben? He wasn't coming back. Life would never be the same.

"Patrick," she said as she stumbled forward. "I can't go on. I have to rest."

"You're right," he said, looking around. It had stopped snowing for the most part, but now it seemed even colder. "It's almost completely dark. It's stupid of me to keep pushing us. I just thought, if there was any way we could make it, that we ought to get down this mountain." He paused and took in a deep breath of air. "Getting home sounds so good to me."

"It's not a stupid idea to try to get down. But

I can't keep following. That's what I'm trying to tell you. I have to rest."

"Okay," he said. "It's going to be too dark to do much else. Let's find a good place to stay the night. If we get down a little ways, there'll be more trees. Maybe I'll be able to find a ridge of snow before it completely freezes for the night and make a snow cave for protection."

Olivia nodded. She couldn't take much more. She felt beyond exhaustion, beyond thinking, in some ways even beyond needing sleep. Her face felt frozen in place. She had no idea what kept her moving.

Suddenly a tree branch that Patrick had been holding back for her flipped across her chest, scraping against the nylon of her parka. "Sorry," Patrick said.

"Didn't hurt," she mumbled. Her head and lips felt too frozen to talk, too frozen to hurt, even. But she was glad they were below timberline. She felt safer already, more protected.

"Olivia." Patrick stopped.

"Yeah?" She hoped this was where they were going to bivouac for the night.

"There is one way we can still get home tonight," he said. "It means taking a big chance. But it's less of a danger now that it's almost nightfall, and cold."

"This is all one big chance as far as I can tell. So what do you have in mind?" The idea of getting home and into her own bed had a refreshing effect. She felt more awake, more herself.

Ben would want them to get home. Ben would want the best for them.

"There's an avalanche chute up ahead," Patrick said. "We could glissade down. Now that everything's pretty much frozen the chute is a lot less dangerous than it was this morning with the sun out. Do you know how to glissade? It's kind of like skiing in your climbing boots. You just glide right down."

"We practiced at the top of Mt. Alabaster two summers ago. I got the hang of it. But it was fun then, Patrick. There was sun out, and not the slightest possibility of an avalanche. We were way up at the top and we had ice axes to slow ourselves if we fell."

"I know you can do it. I'll go ahead and test things out. If the snow holds me without causing a slide, you'll be fine. I won't shoot straight down. That way you won't lose sight of me. I'll only go about fifty yards and pull off to the side. I'll signal and wait for you to catch up. We'll keep doing that. Fifty yards at a time. Okay?"

"As long as I can keep you in sight."

"We'll stay together. Don't worry."

"Don't go beyond that curve down there," she made a point of telling Patrick when they got right to the edge of the chute. It panicked her to see that curve. He could disappear around it in no time. Disappear just as Ben had done. What would she do then? "Are you sure this is right?" She was sorry to keep questioning him but it all seemed too risky.

"I think we ought to try to get home. I'm not sure what kind of chance we have if we have to stay out here tonight. I'll be careful. And I'll wait for you. I won't let us get separated."

She believed him, but as she watched him inch out, and leave her, she wanted to pull him back.

Patrick started down at a steep angle across the open area of the avalanche chute and, once into the sparse woods on the other side, signaled to Olivia and waited for her to begin her trek. Come on, he thought. What's keeping her? He hated the thought of having to go back to get her. That would be an awful struggle. He should never have left her like that.

Maybe she had simply backed up and disappeared like Ben. No, he told himself forcefully. They were nowhere near a cliff when he took off. And she knew better than to start heading in some other direction all by herself. She knew better — unless she was sick and confused. He could kick himself for not reading the signs. Where was she?

He could not afford to yell out. A sudden sharp sound like that was all this kind of snow needed to start moving. So he headed back across the field.

When he was about a third of the way over, he saw her begin to head out above him. Whether the snow could take both of them was his immediate concern. It had taken his weight, and Olivia was light as a bird. He couldn't risk yelling to her to head back.

He heard it before he saw it, the roar of snow

breaking off above them, sounding like a clap of thunder deep inside the snow, a moment later the snow under his very feet seeming to growl and groan. The snow ten yards above him cracked with the noise and started to slip downhill in a line all the way across the chute. "Slide off, Olivia," he screamed up at her. She'd have a better chance than he since she was higher. "Head back to the trees. Avalanche!" He watched her pause. And then he saw the billowing clouds tumbling behind her, as she all but flew back toward the pines. A wall of snow slid in slow motion. Huge chunks, as big and deadly as four-wheel-drive vehicles flung off a cliff, churning downhill. She was gobbled from sight. He took off, headed back toward the edge of the chute that he had just left.

If you're lucky, Patrick, awfully lucky, you'll outride this snowy torrent. But he knew it was hardly likely he'd glissade out of the pathway of the snow that grabbed at him like a human hungry monster.

In seconds he was tossed into the air. The full impact of the load from above hit and completely engulfed him, tearing the walking stick from his tight-fisted grip. Fool! he thought. Fool to have ever thought it was smart to go mountain climbing before June. Fool to think you had a shot at getting back before dark. Fool, fool, fool!

His heart emptied and his lungs closed, as if a tidal wave had hit and he was being swept under, his breath sucked away. Now he felt only panic.

The size of the avalanche was monumental. Ben's face flashed before his eyes. He was going to die, too.

His breath returned, though, as he began to move with the slide. My pack, my pack, he thought. It'll kill me, it'll weigh me down.

But nothing would weigh him down at the speed he was going. He could feel his momentum pick up at an incredible rate. He was twisted here and there, tossed up and down. He didn't have the faintest idea which direction he was going. Every once in a while he could catch a breath of air.

Patrick worked to orient himself, realizing, as he moved downhill faster, which way was up. He maneuvered into a sitting position, with his feet downhill.

He felt the slide slow down. Then it came to a stop. He was still buried and hadn't the faintest idea how deep. It seemed deep.

He started to panic again. No, he told himself. Simply do what's next. He pulled his arms in near his head to make a breathing space for himself. His purest instinct always was survival and the fact that there wouldn't be any rescue team who'd get there in time to save him even if he managed to breathe for a few hours inspired him.

Suddenly the snow gave one last powerhouse push, coming to an abrupt halt. It jolted him. Then he found his head and hands were sticking up out of the snow. He could breathe.

The snow was still moving, very slightly. He strained to keep his mouth and nose up, and began to work his body out. The snow felt as if it had set like cement around his chest and legs. Somehow, some way, he made it. In moments, he was sitting on the surface and able to pull out his feet. His body felt bruised and battered. His pack was nowhere to be seen.

And then he cried to relieve the monumental tension behind his eyes, in his forehead, in every muscle and bone in his body. He felt such exhilaration, too, and thankfulness at having survived. He took a deep breath, shook his head to free his eyes of tears, and looked up. He couldn't even see where he had entered the chute, or where the avalanche had swept him up. He had no idea how many twists and turns they'd taken, the slide and him, how far he'd come, or how on earth to begin to look for Olivia.

"Patrick!" he heard her shout. He had no idea Olivia could shout so loud. He was never so happy to hear anyone in his entire life.

He lumbered up onto the snow and waved his arms. "Here! I'm over here!" he called out, knowing another snowslide was highly unlikely. From his point of view, having ridden down the mountain as he just had, there couldn't possibly be any snow left on top.

He watched Olivia as she ran and fell and ran and crawled her way to him, knowing she was too happy to care about how she made her way through the snow. He headed uphill, slowly, and let her fall into his arms. She was sobbing.

"Did I start it?" she asked.

"With what you weigh? I should have had more

confidence in you, that you were coming. Maybe we set it off, the two of us being on the field together. I don't know. It doesn't matter much. Except, well, what *were* you doing? You seemed to take forever to get started out in the chute and that scared me."

"I was thinking about Ben and about how I don't want to leave him on the mountain by himself. I want to get home, and I don't want to get home."

"I know what you mean."

It was moments before either spoke again. Somehow the outdoors had never seemed so still, so quiet. "There must be a third of the mountain left to go," Olivia said softly.

"Yeah," Patrick agreed. "We've got to set up some kind of camp, where it's protected. And then head out in the morning. At least we have this chute behind us."

"Thank God," Olivia said. "I'm glad you're alive."

"Me, too," he said with one of his big smiles. "And I'll make you a cozy little cave for the night."

"I'll never go to sleep."

"Wait and see. Now, let's really put this chute behind us. Far behind us."

Olivia nodded. "I don't want to leave Ben. But right now there's nothing more I'd like to put behind me than this entire mountain."

As he led the way, Patrick thought about Olivia. He thought about her a lot. They would always have something special between them because of this climb, though he supposed it might be grounds for staying away from each other, too, to avoid remembering what had happened today. He wanted to talk to her about staying friends, but he had to think of how to say what he meant. Now was not the time. Right now the two of them had to get out of this alive. "There's a snowdrift up ahead," he said. "I'll build one of my emergency snow caves."

Patrick worked on the entryway while Olivia rummaged through her pack for food. There was a little coffee left, but it wouldn't get them any warmer. And they wouldn't be able to start a fire because Patrick's supply of waterproof matches was in his lost pack. At least they had light from Olivia's flashlight. Olivia found the jar of hand cream she always brought with her outdoors and gave the lid to Patrick to use as a shovel. It sped things up.

Olivia took over. Patrick held the beam of light now that it was almost completely dark and pushed away the snow as she scooped it out. Their entry went into the drift about three feet and then headed up. She began making the good-sized floor of their sleeping area above the top of the entry just as Patrick explained. That would trap warm air inside. She carefully smoothed and molded the upper surfaces of their sleeping quarters so that any melting snow would run down the walls rather than drip on them. Patrick was wet enough as it was. In doing all this she felt like a pioneer woman, making things as safe and sound as conditions allowed.

Then Patrick worked from the outside in the chilly light offered by the stars and nearly full moon behind a thin shield of swiftly passing clouds. She worked from the inside with the light from her flashlight to make a ventilation hole. After all they'd been through it would hardly be fitting to die in their sleep of asphyxiation. They agreed that whenever either of them woke they'd check the ventilation hole, make sure it hadn't frozen over, and enlarge it if it was becoming too warm inside.

"I'll never be too warm again in my entire life," Olivia said as she huddled next to Patrick inside their little home, a blue glow all around as her flashlight lit up the snowy ice. He put his arms around her and she leaned her head against his shoulder. "Are you okay?" she asked.

"This waterproof jacket kept the snow off me pretty well, and my feet . . . well, I think they were frostbit a long time ago."

"Patrick! No! Take off your boots immediately." They laughed at how, in the tiny space, he struggled to remove his boots. She massaged his feet then, glad they weren't so damaged with frostbite that he'd have to go on like that. Sometimes, to make sure a person got down a mountain, you just let them go on with the frostbite. Otherwise, once thawed out, their feet could hardly stand the pain of walking.

In moments, it seemed, he fell asleep. She slithered out of one of her sweaters and wrapped his feet in the dry wool, then held the bundle that was his feet in her hands. She thought of Walt,

96

safe and sound, but worrying. Don't worry, Walt, she thought. We'll be home soon. She tried to imagine what he might be doing. But she had lost any sense of time.

Her chest shuddered as she thought of all the dark that enveloped her and Patrick. And Ben. Her eyes filled with tears. In moments she was asleep.

CHAPTER

10

As soon as Nat tipped the ball toward the Tarenton basket and into Andrew Poletti's outstretched arms, getting the game with Garrison off to a good start, Mrs. Engborg headed for her office. When she came back fifteen minutes later, word traveled quickly down the cheerleaders' bench, and then to the basketball players, that Patrick, Olivia, and Ben had not been seen at any one of the three area hospitals. Nor were they at the police station. The forest rangers at Winchester Peak had seen Patrick that morning, but no one since.

The phone connection to the ranger station was bad, but Mrs. Engborg heard enough to know that there had been several avalanches on the mountain that day what with the warm sun in the morning followed by the heavy and quick buildup of snow. There was no easy way to break this news to her cheerleaders, so she decided to confer first with Mrs. Oetjen, the school principal, who made it a point to attend all games.

Mary Ellen watched Mrs. Engborg motion to get Mrs. Oetjen's attention. She couldn't help but wonder what their coach knew but wouldn't tell them. If the climbers weren't at a hospital, then they were simply on their way home. Something unavoidable had held them up. That was all there was to it. Mary Ellen repeated this to herself time and again, until the game in front of her became a blur.

"We're losing, Melon," Angie whispered, nudging her from her thoughts. "Don't you think we ought to do a cheer? And pass the word to the crowd that we're cheering for the climbers. Everyone knows now that they're in trouble."

Mary Ellen nodded. She didn't like hearing the word *trouble*. But it was true. They'd be home by now if things were right. Just because they weren't in a hospital didn't mean a thing. Right now she'd give anything to have them in a hospital. "You spread the word, Angie. You and Pres."

They were the two least touched by what was happening. Mary Ellen didn't hold that against them. A crisis seemed to even up everything and everyone. It didn't seem right that it would take a crisis to heal differences and make her love flow more freely. She felt with all her heart that she loved Patrick. She could always be by his side, if she could feel as she did right now. Maybe it was possible.

She watched Angie and Pres move through

the bleachers, spreading the word that they were cheering for the climbers. She could see the news spread across the gym, through the Garrison fans. They grew quiet with the news.

Fear was everywhere. She could feel it. Cutting into everyone and everything.

"Out on the floor," she yelled as soon as Angie and Pres were back in their places. "We're only two points down, but we've got to get way back on top and stay there." Garrison had called a time-out, and so their timing couldn't have been better. They might be short some of their best people with Ben and Olivia missing, but there was no way Tarenton was going to lose this game. "This cheer is for the climbers," Mary Ellen yelled through her megaphone. The fans stood, pompons and Tarenton banners waving from their outstretched arms. "Ben and Olivia," she shouted. "And Patrick." Her voice cracked.

Pres came to her side. "I'm okay," Mary Ellen assured him. Any attention would only make her falter all the more.

"Who's the best?" Mary Ellen asked the crowd.

"We're the best!" the fans boomed back, Walt, Nancy, Pres, and Angie responding with them as they did their daring shoulderstands and handspring combinations.

"Better than the rest?" she asked.

"The best! The best! Better than the rest!"

From that they went into their "Pride" and "Tiger" cheers, racing back to their bench just as play began again. But the Tarenton fans would not sit down easily.

A referee stopped the game, taking the ball from Andrew Poletti. He waved for silence. Mrs. Oetjen came out onto the court and pulled the referee aside. While she talked he nodded and shrugged. Then he blew his whistle shrilly. Rather than play resuming, though, he shouted at the crowd, "Mrs. Oetjen wants to make an announcement."

"I know you are all concerned about the rumor of some of our students missing on a climb. I'll fill you in on the details, everything I know, at halftime. In the meantime, you must remember that the referees need your cooperation, or they won't be able to continue this game." Mrs. Oetjen motioned for the crowd to be a little more quiet. Slowly the fans resumed their seats. Play began again, Nat tipping in a ball and bringing Tarenton to a tie with Garrison.

Nancy clapped her hands, but her throat was too tight to cheer. It was hard to watch the game, harder than anything she'd ever done. Every play, every player, every whistle, every score, reminded her of Ben. Ben and his excellence. She didn't know how to describe him any other way.

Nat was Ben's best friend, and he was really outdoing himself tonight. He usually wasn't a high scorer, though he was the best guard on the team. Ben had that kind of effect on his friends, she thought as she watched Nat. He made people do their best.

She couldn't think like this any longer. But he kept coming back to her, making her more and more afraid of what might have happened. What he might have done. He was daring. He could even be foolhardy.

It didn't help, either, that this was a game with Garrison. He'd played for Garrison when they first met.

"They're probably out there rescuing Olivia," Nancy blurted out. It seemed easier to blame Olivia than to go on remembering how daring Ben could be, that maybe he had pushed them to go further than they should and that he was the reason why everyone was worried.

"What?" Angie asked. "Have you heard something we haven't?"

"No," Nancy mumbled. "Just making a guess. They should never have taken her."

"I don't think that's fair, Nancy," Angie said. "There's no reason to blame anyone."

"What's the matter?" Walt asked. He was seated next to Angie, but had been paying close attention to Nancy all night. Because of how his own feelings about Olivia had welled up during the game, he had grown even more concerned about Nancy. It was next to impossible to get out on the court and cheer without Olivia.

"I just don't think the guys should have taken Olivia," Nancy explained. "You've got to agree with me. She isn't strong enough for this kind of weather."

"We can't keep reliving this," Walt said sternly.

"They took Olivia because, when it comes to being dependable and a disciplined athlete, there's no one better. She's strong, all right. You ought to take a few lessons in the kind of strength she's got." He was angry. He knew he should have kept his last comment to himself. He wanted to be helpful, not critical of Nancy. But to blame Olivia was wrong. He turned his back on Nancy and watched the last minute of the first half as if nothing else mattered to him.

Angie reached out and took his hand. "Come on, Walt. Let's not turn against each other. You, either, Nancy." She took Nancy's hand. "You've both got to be feeling something I can't even begin to feel, with someone you love missing. We've got to stay together over this. We've got to keep going. And keep cheering."

"You have to get out of your huddle," Mrs. Engborg suddenly interrupted them, "if you want to do a halftime show. Mrs. Oetjen's going to make an announcement in a few minutes, right before play begins."

"About what?" Mary Ellen asked.

Mrs. Engborg paused. "You must promise me you'll get out there and cheer just the same." She looked at them expectantly. Each of her cheerleaders nodded.

"We want to know," Walt said. "Good or bad."

"Yeah," Pres agreed. "Whatever the news, it affects us a lot more than anyone else. Patrick and Mary Ellen, Nancy and Ben, Walt and Olivia. . . ."

"I know," Mrs. Engborg said. "That's why I feel I should tell you myself."

"Students." Suddenly Mrs. Oetjen was at the microphone. "I know you're used to a halftime show now. And I was going to wait to talk to you, but the referees have just told me they want the next half to start on time and think it's best I tell you now, so things have a chance to settle down."

The gym went silent. Not a single ball bounced, not another soft drink was poured, not another word whispered.

"I think you all know by now that three of our students here at Tarenton are missing. Ben Adamson, one of our best basketball players, who should be here with the team tonight. Olivia Evans, one of our cheerleaders. And Patrick Henley, a real genius with a camera, especially at sports events like this one. They should all be here. But, as far as we know, they're still on Winchester Peak."

A buzzing murmur went through the crowd.

"We've checked the hospitals and police station. And we've spoken with the rangers out there at the base of the peak. Apparently there were several avalanches sighted there today. . . ."

Nancy slid to the floor, Pres reaching out to grab her just before she crumpled. Mary Ellen sat down, still too full of disbelief to do what she wanted to do, and that was to cry. Angie gasped and turned to Walt.

"No!" Walt shouted. "It can't be." Then he sat down on the bench and buried his face in his hands. "I don't believe it," he muttered. "I won't believe it."

Mrs. Engborg came up to Walt and sat beside him. "None of us wants to believe it," she said. "But it's true. It's what I found out when I made my calls."

The gym had filled with the same sounds and cries as the ones that instinctively came from the cheerleaders. Most of the pompon squad was weeping. Parents and teachers were very distraught. The faces of all the basketball players, both Tarenton and Garrison, were stunned.

Mrs. Oetjen, still at the microphone, looked as if she was having to do the hardest thing she'd ever done during her tenure as principal. "I have more to say," she went on, her voice unsteady. "We are going to finish this game. We are going to play with the kind of spirit these young people — Ben, Olivia, and Patrick — have always shown. To help us do that, I think a moment of silence is in order."

Some heads bowed. Others continued to stare ahead into space. Mary Ellen looked at her brightly painted red nails. She thought of Patrick. She needed comfort. But more than anything, she wished she could give him half the caring and comfort right now he'd ever shown her.

"Now," Mrs. Oetjen said, "let's play ball."

There was a stampede of cheers and clapping. The players rushed out onto the court.

"Mary Ellen! Oh, Mary Ellen!" It was Gemma. She threw her arms around her older sister. "It's going to be okay. I know it."

Finally, Mary Ellen could sob. She buried her head in her sister's shoulder. Angie made room for the two of them on the bench, forcing a Kleenex into Mary Ellen's fist. Gemma patted her sister's lovely long blonde hair, whispering something into her ear. Mary Ellen cried even harder.

Pres turned away. There was something about all this that made him love people, really care about them. Maybe it was that in a crisis people could show their true colors. Like Mary Ellen. When had he ever seen her soften up enough to cry? When had he ever, in his life, seen such a display of sisterly affection as that between Mary Ellen and Gemma? He didn't really need anyone to hug, but he wished Claudia had been able to come to the game. She'd understand what was happening here, and it would be a big help just to look up into the stands and see her eyes looking back at him.

Mrs. Engborg was taking care of Nancy now, gently talking to her. Nancy was trembling.

"It's okay if you want to cry, too, Mrs. Engborg," Pres told her. "I'll sit with Nancy."

"Thank you, but I most certainly will not cry, Pres Tilford," she told him. "Not until I know there's reason to cry."

"Good for you," Walt said. He had fought back tears, too. "I can't cry until I know there's reason to cry. Crying won't help them."

"Hey!" Pres yelled as Nat made another basket. "We're up by ten. We're going to win this game."

"I've got to cheer," Walt said. "That's the

only way I'm going to make it through this game."

"I didn't put an end to cheering," Mrs. Engborg said. "But the crowd understands the point Mrs. Oetjen was making. The crowd doesn't need cheerleaders right now, if you'd rather sit out."

Nancy shook her head, breaking away from Mrs. Engborg's comforting hold. "I need to cheer, too. Even if I feel like a truck hit me. Maybe there isn't reason to cry. Maybe things will work out okay."

"Yeah," Angie said. "Come on, Mary Ellen. They may walk in the door any minute. You'd want them to see your famous smile, wouldn't you?"

"She's got the kind of smile that will earn a million dollars someday," Gemma said, coaxing her sister to take back her role as captain.

"I feel as if I'm in some kind of bad dream," Mary Ellen said. Her tear-stained cheeks were enough to soften even the hardest heart. "I don't believe what's happened."

"We don't know the full story," Walt said. "Come on. Let's cheer like the rest. If they're not back when the game's over, then we'll commiserate over at Angie's. Maybe they'll look for us there."

That seemed to perk up everyone's spirits, and in ten seconds, after a nod from Mary Ellen, the squad was on the floor, doing the best it could under the circumstances.

CHAPTER

What woke Olivia was water dripping onto her nylon parka. A drop landed on her nose, making it itch. She rubbed it, only to feel scratchy, wet wool against her nose. Her mittens were drenched. Warm, but drenched. The cave seemed stifling. This idea of Patrick's really did work. She wondered what time it was.

Olivia still was not sure she wanted to go home. How could they ever explain the accident? Wouldn't everyone, everywhere, blame them? Wouldn't they be talked about the way that people who had committed some crime were? Someone, ready to start in with some gossip, would say, "There goes Olivia Evans, one of the climbers who was on that climb of Winchester Peak three years ago. . . ." And so the story would go.

How would they ever tell Ben's parents? What were the Adamsons thinking now? That their son was safe, probably. Who would ever expect things to have turned out so badly.

She would remember the moment when she last saw Ben for the rest of her life. Seeing him, and then not seeing him.

Olivia didn't want to wake Patrick. He'd been through so much. How he lived through that avalanche she'd never know. But something seemed not right. The air in the cave, maybe. She sure felt sick. She felt drowsy. Her eyes burned. Without the flashlight on, the cave offered absolutely no light. Even with water dripping the way it was — from a faucet in her home it would have driven her crazy — didn't bother her. No. In fact, the constant sound felt comforting. The water on her face felt warm.

Time to sleep, she told herself. I need to rest up for the long walk back. Even if she'd wanted to fight sleep, there was nothing she could do but let the warm drowsiness overtake her.

Patrick was dreaming about Mary Ellen's long blonde hair and how it felt like satin to him. Such a luscious, golden satin. He reached out to touch her hair.

Then he was awake. Everything felt wet. And suffocating. He remembered the snow cave. Hadn't he made an air vent? Sure he had. But something was wrong.

And where was Olivia? He reached out and found her. He could not shake her awake.

Patrick felt disoriented. He couldn't remember where he was in relation to the entry way he knew they'd made. Everything that had frightened him about the avalanche came back to him, and he wondered if another one had happened while they'd been asleep.

"Olivia!" he shouted. He shook her again. She slid slightly along the wet, hardpacked snow floor. Then it all began to come back to him. He crawled over her, rummaging for his hiking boots. When he had them, he inched his way backward, through the entry tunnel, dragging her feet first behind him. He broke through into blinding light and fresh air.

It's a sunny day, he thought. He wanted that to be enough to make him celebrate. He wanted to take time to say thanks, to turn his face to the sun, to enjoy the mountain just like always. He loved the sun. He always would. But something had been lost. A sunny day didn't make everything fine, as it had before. Sunshine wasn't enough.

Olivia was still unconscious. Her lips were a little bluish and her breathing was shallow. The air vent must have frozen shut as we slept, Patrick thought. She needs air. He sprinkled some of the fluffy white snow from yesterday's storm on her cheeks and forehead.

"Patrick?" It was Olivia. She opened her eyes and squinted. She was breathing, breathing just as usual. She was with him. "Patrick, I don't feel so good. I have to throw up but I don't want to. I don't want to spoil our cave."

"Go ahead. You're outside now. It'll make you feel better."

"I hate throwing up in front of people," she explained as she rolled over.

He laughed. "You worry about the silliest things, Olivia Evans. After all we've been through, the two of us have nothing to hide." He waited till she was feeling better. Then he picked her up, gently swinging her around and onto his shoulders, and headed down the mountain.

Patrick could see the ranger station from the crest. They had a good half-mile hike left. Then he heard a helicopter. There was a rescue mission underway. Suddenly he realized how much publicity there would be about what had happened.

In some ways, it seemed as if the struggle was just beginning. A different kind of struggle. How would he ever tell Ben's parents? Or Nancy? All he wanted was to go home and crawl into his bed and not come out for days. He wanted to forget all about the climb, for a while anyway. But he knew that was not possible. He'd grown up on the mountain behind him. And lost something, too. A kind of innocence. They'd never have Ben again. And Patrick would never be the same again.

"Are you stuck?" Olivia asked from her perch. "Or just enjoying the scenery? It's okay with me. I'm just wondering why we stopped and what's going on. You never know around here."

Patrick laughed lightly and squeezed Olivia's leg. "You just never know, do you?"

"You never do."

There was a lightness between them, a sense

111

of humor as they made their final descent. It felt like a kindness for each other. That's the best way Patrick could explain it. He figured he and Olivia would always have that between them.

Patrick slipped a few feet but caught himself.

"Hey, watch it!" Olivia said. "You've got valuable merchandise here."

He smiled. "Darn right."

There was a movement off to the left and then someone shouted, "Hey, I think we've found them!" Two rangers came through the brush. "You the kids that are lost?" one of them asked.

"Not anymore," Patrick said.

CHAPTER

 12

"Pretty ingenious," the forest ranger who'd introduced himself as Ed Swanson commented when Patrick had finished telling the story of the avalanche, and then the snow cave. The rangers had put Olivia on a toboggan and phoned ahead for an ambulance. She was probably down the hill by now. The rangers thought she'd probably need hospitalization for exposure, maybe shock, at least for observation purposes.

"At least we've heard the last of Mrs. Evans," Ed said, when they were within fifty feet of the ranger station. Ed explained that she'd been calling them, and the police, every hour on the hour. "Ever since that Manners kid told her where Olivia was."

"She's probably the type to sue," the other ranger said.

"She's got no cause," Patrick said. "You guys did warn us."

"Your dad's here, Patrick," announced another ranger, stepping from the cabin.

There, over the ranger's shoulders, Patrick could see his father. He was sipping a cup of coffee. Their eyes met. "Dad!" Patrick shouted.

"Son," his father said, grabbing him in a big bear hug. "I knew you'd make it."

"One of the others didn't, Dad."

"Later, Patrick. It can wait till later."

Patrick felt that his dad and the forest rangers had made coming home easy for him. They cared, and they'd all done enough mountaineering to understand what he and Olivia had been through. They were gentle with him, calling Ben's parents and not putting him through that ordeal, though he knew he had things he wanted to say to them. He just had to figure out how.

"But I've got to be the one to tell Nancy," he told them. Nancy was a friend. And she had loved Ben. The way he loved Mary Ellen.

After the rangers had made all their calls, to Mrs. Evans and the Adamsons, to the police and highway department, he called Mary Ellen, only to find out that all the cheerleaders were still at Angie's. "They've been there all night waiting, Patrick," Gemma explained. "Boy, is it good to hear your voice."

Patrick's hands trembled as he gripped the steering wheel of his truck. It felt strange to be back in civilization.

Suddenly Patrick wished he'd let his father come along, instead of telling him to go home and tell his mom he'd be home soon. No, he told himself, I can do it.

He didn't even bother to knock, or ring the bell at Angie's. The Polettis never stood on formality, and certainly wouldn't today.

"Patrick!" Angie screamed. It was easy to tell she wanted to race into his arms, but she held back and looked at Mary Ellen. Mary Ellen jumped to her feet.

Patrick looked at Mary Ellen and shook his head. She knew right away that something was wrong. Her mouth opened in that way it did when she was frightened. He wanted to kiss her and make everything okay. But things were not okay.

Out of the corner of his eyes, Patrick could see Pres and Walt. They were all still in their cheerleading uniforms. Then he found Nancy, curled up like a cat in the corner of the sofa. She watched every move he made as he walked toward her. Slowly she unwound from her curl and stood up.

"What is it, Patrick?" she asked, reaching out to take his hand.

He knew she knew. She didn't say how good it was to see him. Her hands were ice cold, and she had turned white. She grabbed at him, falling against his chest, clutching at his arms for support. He held her. "Ben didn't come back with us," he said, his voice cracking. "It was an accident, Nancy. Nothing but an accident. He's dead." He couldn't think of anything else to say. Why hadn't he planned his speech better?

He could hear Angie gasp, and sink back onto the couch.

Patrick could feel Nancy tremble. He kissed her hair and stroked her head. She started to cry, her body wracked with her hard sobs. At first, she sounded like a wounded animal, or a yelping puppy. Then her cries deepened and she completely collapsed against him. Patrick felt he had to take hold of someone. He wasn't sure he could make it through this flood of emotion.

And Mary Ellen was there in an instant, kissing his shoulder, her arm snug around his waist. There was nothing to say, and he appreciated that she didn't try to find something to say. He just wanted her with him.

"Olivia?" Walt asked from the daze he'd been put into by the news. "Where's Olivia?"

"She's okay, isn't she?" Angie asked.

Patrick nodded. "She's at the hospital for observation. They want to check her for shock and exposure." Walt collapsed on a chair behind the group, lost in his own thoughts and feelings.

Patrick started to tell the cheerleaders the story of their climb, but when he got to their stop for lunch, explaining how the blizzard had taken them completely by surprise, he began to cry. "We couldn't save him, Nancy. Nothing. . . ." But he just couldn't go on.

* * *

116

Olivia was admitted to the hospital, checked for vital signs, and placed in a private room, something she requested. She didn't want to have to talk to strangers, and she didn't really want to talk at all. She wanted to enjoy being alive, enjoy how warm she felt, enjoy being alone with nothing to do but be taken care of. For the first time in her life, she didn't mind being in a hospital.

Being in a hospital, even for one day, gave her some kind of protection. She wanted to feel safe and secure before heading out into the world that would ask her question after question, demanding an explanation, or at least a thorough recounting, of what had happened.

As Olivia was lying in her bed, staring out the broad hospital window at the bright day outside, she had two visitors in rapid succession. First her mom bustled in, ordering around nurses, even the intern making his rounds, before she broke the news to Olivia.

"I have never been so humiliated," she began, choosing not to look Olivia in the face. "My own daughter off on some mountain, with avalanches all over the place, and who's the last to know? Her mother."

"I didn't tell Daddy either."

Olivia and her mother talked back and forth about everything, but, to Olivia's way of thinking, nothing. She watched as her mom rearranged everything in the room, even getting on a chair to try to dust the TV that was suspended from the ceiling. When a flower arrangement came in, Mrs. Evans laid claim to it and began rearranging the daisies.

"Who are they from?" Olivia asked. They were from Claudia Randall. Nothing seemed so strange to Olivia as to get flowers from Claudia before even seeing Walt. Pres must have called her right away.

After Mrs. Evans left, Vanessa walked in. "You look like the cat who just swallowed a canary," Vanessa said, closing the door behind her and sauntering to a large stuffed chair at the foot of Olivia's bed. She was wearing expensive leather boots in a lovely shade of rust, a long black split skirt with a white silk blouse, and a black vest with heavy braid.

"And you look very Spanish," Olivia retorted. "You ought to have a rose in your mouth."

Vanessa laughed. "That would be more stunning, I suppose, than those drippy-looking daisies. Did Walt send those?"

"No. They're from Claudia. I had my mother take Walt's home. They're the most beautiful collection of — " She was going to expand on her little lie, but Vanessa interrupted.

"I'm sure, I'm sure," Vanessa said. "My dad sent me to see you and wish you well. But as superintendent, he feels he needs a full report of what happened. So he sent me. Besides, since I'm dating Nat and he was Ben's best friend, I feel sort of part of the family, and that I have an obligation to my dad to get the facts. *All* the facts."

"Sure, Vanessa. It's no secret. It'll all be in the paper."

"I need a personal account, though. My dad wants this to be accurate. Just in case he has some explaining to do to the Adamsons."

"Why would he have any explaining to do?"

Vanessa bit the end of her pencil. "Well, there's a rumor that the Adamsons will sue the school. Apparently, Ben told them he was climbing as part of an exercise for a school club."

"Oh, no," Olivia said right away. "That isn't true. We were thinking of starting one. That's all."

"See," Vanessa said. "Things are being reported wrong already. We know there's no mountain climbing club at school, but we need to make sure it wasn't you or Patrick who led him to believe that's why he was making this climb."

"You mean we're going to get sued?"

"I hadn't thought about that, but I suppose they could sue you and Patrick. People sue over everything these days."

"But we're just kids."

"You're kids who had an accident on a mountain and someone got killed. That's not your everyday kind of occurrence. Wouldn't you agree?"

"I guess," Olivia said as she watched Vanessa begin to take down what she said, word for word. "Accidents like this do happen, though."

"If my writing makes you nervous," Vanessa said, "we can tape this conversation. I brought a tape."

Olivia thought for a minute. "Sure. Maybe that would be better." She didn't trust how Vanessa could twist her words. She didn't trust Vanessa, period, but if Dr. Barlow had sent her, and if all this litigation could happen, Olivia would have to talk to somebody, sometime. She'd just as soon get it over with.

Vanessa reached into her large black leather shoulder bag. "Before we start — are there going to be any cute interns coming into this room?"

Olivia shrugged. "Depends on what you think is cute."

"Just don't blow my cover if I talk like I'm a reporter with the *Tarenton Lighter*, okay? I am doing you a favor taking care of this report right away."

"It doesn't feel like a favor, but I don't care what sort of games you play with men. Just don't play any games with me, Vanessa, okay?"

"Don't worry. There's a whole ethical code to being a reporter."

Olivia was still worried. But she started in on the story, beginning with Patrick's picking her up.

"No," Vanessa said. "You have to go all the way back to the beginning. When the three of you planned the trip. What you promised each other, what you expected."

Oh, where was Walt? She needed a kiss and a hug. She needed to be holding him. She hoped he hurried. He had to know by now that she was in the hospital. "Let me make one phone call," Olivia said.

"Sure. They even let criminals make one phone call."

"Oh, forget it." Olivia hated the inferences Vanessa was making. And if she was tough enough to make it on the mountain without Walt, she could tough it out a little longer without him by her side. He'd get there when he got there.

CHAPTER

The cheerleaders, minus Nancy, poured into Olivia's room, the intern on duty protesting loudly. Olivia was explaining to Vanessa how she'd passed out in the snow cave.

"What's going on here?" Walt wanted to know. He was carrying at least a dozen yellow roses in one hand, red roses in the other. Olivia felt she had never been so glad to see anyone in her entire life.

"That's what I want to know," the intern said, looking accusingly at the cheerleaders. "Olivia shouldn't have this many visitors here at one time."

"We're her friends," Angie explained.

"My best friends," Olivia said.

"And I'm here doing a little reporting," Vanessa said, taking the doctor's arm. "Wouldn't you like to tell me your involvement in this heartrending story?" In seconds she had him out the door.

"What was that all about?" Walt asked.

"Don't ask," Olivia insisted. "Hug." She reached out her arms.

"Anything you say." Walt handed the flowers to Mary Ellen and reached for Olivia. She felt light as air, as usual. But something was different. Maybe it was just that he was so happy, so thankful, to hold her. "I was so scared," he whispered in her ear.

"You think *you* were scared," she murmured back. "Don't leave when the others go. Please. I want to sit and hold your hand."

He nodded. Then they went back to group visiting. Everyone had heard the story, so Olivia didn't have to repeat herself. Patrick and Nancy were visiting with the Adamsons. "They're real understanding about the whole thing," Walt said. "I mean they're hurt and upset. But there's not an ounce of blame in them, for you or Patrick."

"We didn't do anything wrong," Olivia said.

"I know," Walt said. "Patrick said Ben had enough experience but he just slipped. Or maybe he was out on a ledge that had built up because of the new snow and it broke off with his weight."

"It was an accident, for sure. But Vanessa said the Adamsons were going to sue."

"Vanessa's full of hot air," Walt said. "She just likes to stir up trouble. Even when there's more than enough to go around as it is." They all started talking then about Nancy, and what they might be able to do to help her.

Mary Ellen felt more separated from Patrick once he came home than when he was on the mountain. He was so in demand, by the police, by the forest service, by the Adamsons, by Nancy, by Olivia, by the press. He became almost a celebrity, though she could tell he wanted no part of it. He'd even been part of the rescue operation that had lifted Ben's body from the mountain. And Ben's family had asked him to read something about the spirit of mountaineering at Ben's funeral on Wednesday.

Patrick was so busy on Sunday, and again on Monday, that it was Tuesday, while he was going over what the Adamsons wanted him to read at the funeral the next day, before he had a chance to feel all that was inside of him. Damn! He should have done more. He should have done something differently. Ben would be alive if Patrick had been a good enough leader. He should have headed down the mountain earlier. He knew Ben liked adventure and exploring. He should have taken that more into account and put him second, Olivia bringing up the rear.

Damn you, Ben! reeled through his mind. You jerk! Why'd you have to die and go and leave us.

But even as the anger at Ben surged in him, he felt guilty. Guilty about being angry at Ben and guilty that he hadn't been the kind of leader Ben needed. A lot of good all that mountain training had been. What had he done wrong?

He looked at the book of poetry Mrs. Adamson had given him with the selection he was to read. It was then that Patrick broke down and sobbed, his tears wetting the passage, his fists clenched and halfheartedly pounding against his desk.

There was nothing any of them could do at the funeral to comfort Nancy, especially after Patrick read his poem. Nancy wanted to be left alone afterward, but Angie felt that wasn't right. They should at least be with her, even if they didn't say anything that helped. How could anyone say anything that would help? Simply being with someone was a message in and of itself.

Angie and her mom had taken a whole meal to the Adamsons. It was a tradition in her family to do that sort of thing, for births and deaths. It was a tradition that said you cared, that said life went on.

Angie thought about all this as she walked home from the funeral with her brother, Andrew, who had his arm protectively around her shoulders.

"There's a rumor going around, Ange, that's making some of the guys on the team angry. I know it's not true, but you cheerleaders are being accused of a cover-up," Andrew told her.

"A cover-up?" Angie asked, completely confused. "What sort of a cover-up?"

"That Ben's fall was all Olivia's fault. That she made Patrick and Ben go on with the climb even when they wanted to back out at the last minute. And then she wasn't strong enough to keep up with the guys. They figure Ben slipped trying to help her. Apparently she was so unsteady she needed a walking stick right from the start. And people say Ben wasn't skilled enough for the climb, but the guys on the team think that's part of the cover-up, too, to take the blame off Olivia."

Angie was astounded. "There's no cover-up. That's an ugly, ugly rumor."

"You and I know that, Angie. But someone's really setting you guys up for trouble. The locker room was really steaming after last night's practice. Whoever's spreading the rumor has heard the whole story. There are so many details, about what happened where and how decisions were made, that it's got to be someone close to you guys."

"Vanessa," she said, slowly.

"Vanessa Barlow? How do you know that?"

Angie told him of Vanessa visiting Olivia and taking a report. "She said it was for her dad. She even taped the whole interview. She said there would be lawsuits against the school, maybe even against Olivia and Patrick, but she and her dad would be able to stop them if they had all the facts."

"That's a bunch of baloney. The Adamsons understand perfectly what happened. They'd never sue."

"Well, Olivia didn't know that. And if Nancy hears the rumor, I don't know what she'll do. She's closed us all out as it is. She just might believe that Ben was a victim. She was ready to blame Olivia, even when we didn't know what had happened when they were late getting back."

"You take care of Nancy," Andrew said. "And I'll take care of the rumor. Nat might know if Vanessa started it. And Patrick's just the guy to help me get it out of him. The school's so hurt by all this already, it shouldn't have to put up with an ugly rumor on top of everything else."

It didn't take much for Patrick and Andrew to get the full story from Nat. "Vanessa told me as if she had all the facts. You know how she is. Being the superintendent's daughter and all, I just figured she knew the *real* story. I couldn't figure out why someone like Ben would slip and fall. None of us can. The way Vanessa explained his death as Olivia's fault, and that the cheerleaders were spreading some rumor about Ben not being skilled enough, to cover up Olivia's role in his fall, made sense. He was captain of the basketball team, you know. He had a lot of talent. A fall like that should never have happened to him. Vanessa's explanation seemed a good one to me."

"Vanessa spreads rumors all the time," Andrew said. "She likes to play it dirty. Especially when it comes to the cheerleaders. You should know that."

"Well, I know she has a reputation. She has a reputation about a lot of things. I just didn't think she'd have the nerve to spread a rumor about something like Ben's death. And her story seemed good."

"It was an accident," Patrick said. He felt ready to explode and it took all the effort he could summon to remain cool. "People like to think they can control everything, but accidents happen in mountain climbing all the time. Especially when the weather goes bad all of a sudden, like it did on us. It had nothing to do with how skilled Ben was. It could have happened to anybody. And it had absolutely nothing to do with Olivia. She was nothing but cautious and careful the whole time, ready to abandon the climb as soon as going on looked like the wrong thing to do. Do you have that straight?"

"Yeah, Patrick," Nat said. "I've got it straight. But don't blame me."

"I really didn't want to get around to putting blame anywhere in this. But now I know exactly where to place the blame. Vanessa," he sputtered. A second later he was out the door.

Nancy wandered the halls of her parents' home. She felt such an emptiness.

Her dad had gone back to work after the funeral. Her mom had to give a lecture at an art showing that couldn't be canceled, or even postponed. Nancy hadn't minded and had told them to go ahead with their plans. They'd been all over her, it felt, with comfort, and it seemed a good idea to be alone for a while. But the emptiness was unbearable. She wished they'd been able to go out for lunch, even, or a walk. Funny, first she was glad to get rid of them. Now she needed them.

The doorbell rang. She thought about not answering it. She didn't have to check a mirror to know her eyes were red. Well, she'd peek out the window first. It was Angie, standing on her doorstep with something covered in aluminum foil. Curious, she opened the door.

"It's probably silly," Angie said right away. "But I thought you might like something to eat. I can hardly imagine how much you're hurting but. . . ."

"Oh, Angie," Nancy exclaimed. Her face couldn't decide whether to smile or cry, and she did both. "It isn't silly at all. You must have read my mind or something. Come in." Nancy led the way to the Goldsteins' large country kitchen, full of yellow and orange. Angie set the dish down on the counter.

Nancy looked at Angie. Then her lips began to quiver. "Oh, Angie."

Angie reached out her arms and Nancy rushed into them. "I don't know how I'll ever get over it," Nancy said. "I feel as if I've got a hole right in the center of my chest. When I close my eyes I see his face." She had her eyes closed now and that was all she saw, Ben's smiling, eager face. "He was so exciting to be with. I'll miss him all my life."

"Sure," Angie said. "How could you not?" Angie paused. "I could kick myself. I haven't the faintest idea what to say to help."

"You've helped," Nancy said. "Just by coming. People don't know what to say about grief, and they avoid you. And I guess I wanted to be avoided, too. It's been so hard to keep it together. But being with you helps. And I think I need to talk. My mom wants to talk but I don't exactly want to talk to her, you know what I mean?"

Angie nodded. "I'm a great listener."

More than anything, Patrick wanted to be with Mary Ellen. But he simply could not stand the thought of Vanessa tearing the school apart with her ugly rumors. That girl had done enough destructive things to last a lifetime. Why did she have to split the school apart with false accusations, when what was important was the loss all of them felt with Ben's death?

He headed straight for Mrs. Oetjen's home. He was going to go to no less than the school principal to get this mess straightened out. And if going through channels didn't get the right response, then Patrick himself would teach Vanessa a lesson that would cure her forever.

Mrs. Oetjen listened attentively as she sat in her living room, Patrick pacing back and forth in front of her. She looked as distraught by the news as Patrick felt. When he finished she reached for the phone on the end table without saying a word. "Carol Ann," she said to the secretary who worked in her office, "I want you to do a little overtime this afternoon. Can you meet me at the office in an hour? Good. I want to issue a suspension order for Vanessa Barlow. Yes. I'm calling her parents now. We can go through the whole hearing procedure. I just want her off school grounds for the rest of the week. I don't care if it's reversed at the hearing." There was a long pause. "Don't worry. I know perfectly well what I'm doing."

Patrick knew, too. Since Dr. Barlow was superintendent of schools, Mrs. Oetjen was placing her job in serious jeopardy.

Mrs. Oetjen looked at Patrick as soon as she hung up. "You're right, Patrick. The school needs something more than a day off to go to Ben's funeral. We need to do something that's special, that captures the spirit of the school, of Ben, and what we thought of him. Have you noticed how hollow the halls are since he died? We need to do something creative — to show what he's meant to us, and so we can go on with our lives."

Patrick nodded. "Sounds like a great idea, Mrs. Oetjen."

"I'm going to call the Barlows now. No sense your being around for that. Meet me in my office in two hours. You don't mind being part of the planning, do you?"

"Are you kidding? I'm just amazed you saw things my way."

She smiled. "Sometimes we adults do understand the important things, you know."

"Well, you've taken care of Vanessa. I think I've got a couple ideas for doing something special for Ben and for the school. And just the people to put them into action."

CHAPTER

14

Olivia was not sure she could go through with what Patrick planned. Saturday night's basketball game against Cedar Point was going to be played in Ben's memory.

And at the game Mrs. Oetjen would announce the beginning of the Ben Adamson Mountaineering Club, funded by the Adamsons to help students not only learn about climbing and outdoor survival, but enjoy and appreciate the beauty and peace of the mountains. Vanessa's sudden disappearance from school the day after Ben's funeral, and the news that she'd been suspended, seemed to make the halls feel less hollow, more warmed by the memory of Ben than chilled by his absence.

Pres and Walt were at Olivia's house, helping Olivia create a special cheer for the game. They were trying to get her approval for all the high-flying gymnastics they wanted her to do. Each time they came up with a new segment, though, she had her doubts.

"I just don't know," she answered Walt, when he finally asked her why she seemed to be resisting all their ideas and suggestions. "It isn't my mother who's making me hesitant. You know my dad's made it a rule that she can't question my judgment when it comes to sports. And I feel fine. The doctor says I'm in as good a condition as before. I don't have to be careful about anything. Even for my mother."

"Then what's wrong?"

"I don't know. I'll get over it. You know what I can do. Just plan the routine. I'll do it." Everyone knew Olivia could do just about anything once she set her mind to it.

There were banners everywhere Saturday night, bright red with white lettering. DO IT FOR BEN, some said. BEN'S WIN, others proclaimed. BEN ADAMSON MEMORIAL BASKETBALL GAME was lettered across the doorway. A booth with information about the mountaineering club was set up near the entrance to the locker rooms. Mr. Adamson, looking very touched by what was happening all around him, sat talking to Mrs. Oetjen.

"Someone from Cedar Point was saying this was the goofiest game he'd ever been to. I almost punched him in the nose," Walt told the cheerleaders as they assembled. He was dancing up and down, more nervous than usual. It was an important game. Everyone wanted a win for Ben.

133

Patrick raced up and hugged Mary Ellen. "Give it your best shot," he said, kissing her lips and then her hair. "Ben deserves our best."

"We've got our best wrapped up in the neatest little routine you've ever seen," Pres told him.

"I don't think I can go out there," Nancy said. "I'm already crying."

"We're going to cry," Mary Ellen said. "How can we avoid it? But we've got to keep going."

"We're here for each other," Angie reminded them. "If it gets too bad, Nancy, lean on one of us."

The Cedar Point players began to warm up, but when the Tarenton team came on the floor, the cheering was so loud, the stomping so intense, that a few players stopped to cover their ears. "For Ben! For Ben!" went up the chant.

Walt's eyes misted over. Olivia reached out and squeezed his hand.

Mary Ellen led the way then, tearing out onto the court. Someone shouted Nancy's name and a cheer went up for her, everyone knowing what she was going through and how much Ben's death hurt. People stood up for her, one by one, clapping till she was forced to move forward.

Instead of simply doing pre-game warm-ups, the cheerleaders led the growing audience in Ben's favorite cheers — the "Growl," "Go for More," and "Catch 'Em While You Can" cheers — ending with the school song that, with its slow refrain, brought most everyone in the gym, including many of the Cedar Point fans, to tears.

Then the game began. Nat made the first basket. He leaped into the air and at the top of his lungs yelled, "Ben!" He punched his fist above him and came down, his feet hopping.

"Ben's Men!" someone in the crowd yelled, and the cheer caught on, fists punching high into the air. "Ben's Men! Ben's Men!" they chanted.

At halftime Mrs. Oetjen made her announcement about the mountaineering club. Mrs. Oetjen then told the crowd there would be a special cheer for Ben at the end of the game to send them out into the night full of the memory of Ben. "A bold boy," Mrs. Oetjen concluded, "who will be missed deeply."

It was the memory of Ben, too, that brought the Tarenton team back on the court completely refreshed for the last half. Andrew Poletti stole the ball the minute it was in play and raced to bring the lead up to seventeen points. They were unstoppable, up to the point that there was a minute left on the clock and Tarenton was ahead by twenty-four points.

All the cheerleaders were crying as the countdown began, crying and cheering. Nancy felt the floor vibrate and listened to the bleachers shake. The Tarenton Wolves raced up and down the court, their pace intense, never slackening. It was how Ben played, always giving everything and everyone his very best, up to the very end.

As she watched the team Ben had so often led to victory, Nancy thought about all the things she wished for Ben. She wished that he'd had a

135

chance to go to college and play basketball there, that he'd had a chance to pass on what he knew to some young, aspiring athlete. That he'd had a full adult life, traveling, seeing mountains everywhere.

The cheerleaders were in a line now, holding hands, giving each other support and encouragement. Mary Ellen nodded them into action just as the clock came to zero. The gym went wild with clapping as the cheerleaders raced to take over the floor. It was time for their final cheer, their cheer for Ben.

Walt spun Olivia round and round. She leaped from his hands into a cartwheel. And then into one handspring after another, leading Angie and Mary Ellen and Nancy down the middle of the court. The girls took their positions in front while Olivia did an almost impossible leap onto Walt's shoulders. From her perch, she began the cheer, motioning for response from the crowd, waving madly at Patrick in the audience.

The entire Tarenton basketball team gathered around the cheerleaders. They flung their fists high into the air, marking the beat to the cheer that Olivia had made up in memory of Ben.

"Ben, Ben, you always
showed your stuff.
One cheer tonight
Will never be enough!"

It was a different kind of cheer. A cheer of

love. And it burst through the Tarenton gym, making its way to Winchester Peak and filling the dark, peaceful sky that only a week before had brought disaster.

Tonight, though, was anything but disaster. Tonight was filled with love and memories of Ben.

Is there a new boy in Angie's life? Read Cheer-leaders #16, IN LOVE.

Join the Team!

They're talented. They're fabulous-looking. They're winners! And they've got what you want! Don't miss any of these exciting CHEERLEADERS books!

Watch for these titles! $2.25 each

☐ QI 33402-6   **Trying Out** *Caroline B. Cooney*
☐ QI 33403-4   **Getting Even** *Christopher Pike*
☐ QI 33404-2   **Rumors** *Caroline B. Cooney*
☐ QI 33405-0   **Feuding** *Lisa Norby*
☐ QI 33406-9   **All the Way** *Caroline B. Cooney*
☐ QI 33407-7   **Splitting** *Jennifer Sarasin*

Books chosen with you in mind from

—Pass the word.

Living...loving...growing.
That's what **POINT** books are all about!
They're books you'll love reading and
will want to tell your friends about.

Don't miss these other exciting Point titles!

NEW POINT TITLES! $2.25 each